THEY CAME TO LAREDO

Owen Pryor—He paid th ... early outlaw days—n... ...can prevent the ... ...ets of Laredo as ... ...er from hanging ...

Molly Bishop— ... ...y young woman carrying a heavy emotio... burden—that only the condemned man can lift.

Bart Campion—A feared outlaw facing execution for killing the Laredo sheriff but confident his men will spill a lot more blood in Laredo to set him free.

Jim Dance—He must choose between the two roads of the law and between the friendship of the man whose life he once saved and the outlaws who will kill him if he betrays them.

The Stagecoach Series

STAGECOACH STATION II:
LAREDO

Hank Mitchum

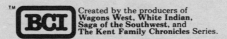

Created by the producers of
**Wagons West, White Indian,
Saga of the Southwest,** and
The Kent Family Chronicles Series.

Executive Producer: Lyle Kenyon Engel

BANTAM BOOKS
TORONTO · NEW YORK · LONDON · SYDNEY

STAGECOACH STATION 11: LAREDO
A Bantam Book / October 1982

Produced by Book Creations, Inc.
Executive Producer: Lyle Kenyon Engel.

ISBN 0-553-14985-7

Published simultaneously in the United States and Canada

Bantam Books are published by Bantam Books, Inc. Its trademark,
consisting of the words "Bantam Books" and the portrayal of a
rooster, is Registered in U.S. Patent and Trademark Office and in
other countries. Marca Registrada. Bantam Books, Inc., 666 Fifth
Avenue, New York, New York 10103.

PRINTED IN THE UNITED STATES OF AMERICA

O   0 9 8 7 6 5

As I walked out in the streets of Laredo,
    As I walked out in Laredo one day,
I spied a poor cowboy wrapped up in white linen,
    All wrapped up in white linen and cold as the clay.

"I see by your outfit that you are a cowboy,"
    These words he did say as I proudly stepped by,
"Come sit down beside me and hear my sad story,
    I'm shot in the breast and I know I must die.

"Then beat the drum slowly, and play the fife lowly,
    And play the dead march as you carry me along.
Take me to the green valley and lay the sod o'er me,
    For I'm a poor cowboy and I know I've done wrong."

STAGECOACH STATION II:
LAREDO

Chapter 1

Owen Pryor was beginning to lose track of the days and the miles, and even the number of times along the way he'd traded for fresh horses. But he was really feeling the distance he'd covered as well as the pressure that seemed to grow with every hour that slipped by. He could hardly believe it now as he saw the tiny huddle of buildings that had begun shaping up in the sun-glare ahead of him, and the long streak of wheel ruts that cut in from the northeast across his route.

They gave him his bearings. The nearer he came, the surer he was that this had to be a station on the stage road south from San Antone.

Once he had figured that out, some part of the fatigue that weighed on him as heavily as the scorching heat of the afternoon sun against his back seemed to slide away. The many miles he had ridden had taken their toll, but having outlasted them he knew now he could manage what remained. Owen Pryor was still a young man, in vigorous good health. A saddle was home to him. It took more than a lengthy journey by horseback to sap his strength for long.

To his thinking there was no lonelier place on God's earth than a stage station, existing for nothing except the few times during the week when one of the coaches pulled in briefly for fresh teams and a hurried meal. Riding in from the chaparral, Pryor made out a few adobe buildings that were the neutral color of the baked mud they had been made from: the station building, a barn, smaller shed, and outhouses. A couple of corrals held the stage-line horses; a live oak made a single spot of greenery, and a hot wind stirred its branches. Someone was working in the blacksmith shed—as he rode nearer he could smell the smoke of the forge and hear the clang of the sledge on heated metal.

Pryor saw a well and made directly for it.

He dismounted stiffly, a wide-shouldered man in a cattle-rancher's well-worn clothing—scuffed boots that were shiny at the ankles from rubbing the stirrup; jeans and neckcloth and faded flannel shirt with black circles of sweat beneath the arms. He took off his hat and batted the dust from it against his knee and hung it on the saddlehorn. He drew up a bucket of well water, drank sparingly, then poured the rest over his head and face and felt better for it. He led the chestnut to the trough, and as the animal drank he wiped his face on his neckcloth and combed the wet strands of thick black hair with his fingers. He had blunt, sun-darkened features with a slash of a black and untrimmed mustache. His face was strong rather than handsome. He put on his hat and looked about the station layout.

He had already noticed at least a dozen men hanging around aimlessly in the scant shade that the lowering sun put in front of the main building. They were a motley bunch, one or two with the look of cowmen, but mostly they wore the varied garb of town dwellers. A bunch had a blanket spread and were hunkered around it playing poker; another lay stretched out with his hat over his face, obviously asleep. There was a murmur of talk, with an angry edge to it. Those men were waiting and from the look of them had grown bored and angry. And then Pryor saw the coach and understood what the situation was.

It was one of Abbot & Downing's big Concords, the sturdy and serviceable vehicle that had first opened the frontier West to transcontinental coach travel. Still today, in the 1870's, they plied the roads wherever the fast-spreading railroads hadn't yet reached. Having ridden in them Owen Pryor could testify that these big coaches were more comfortable than they might look— though built without springs, the heavy leather thoroughbraces on which they were slung managed to absorb the worst punishment of ruts and potholes. But at a glance, he saw this coach had something wrong with it, it stood at an odd kilter. From curiosity he walked over, leading his horse, to get a closer look.

Something seemed to have happened to the steel stanchion anchoring the forward end of the near thoroughbrace. The heavy leather straps hung limp while the coach, unsupported, sagged onto the running gear. Until it could be repaired, this vehicle was out of commission.

"A mess, ain't it?" someone said. A bald-headed man, his face and scalp burned dark brown by the Texas sun, had approached from the direction of the blacksmith shed. He looked sour and frustrated.

"You the station manager?" Pryor asked. Getting a brief nod, he went on, "How did it happen?"

"Who knows? Even good steel will take a notion to break for no reason. Of course, the damn stage was overloaded." He indicated the idlers waiting impatiently in the shade. "She was carrying sixteen, hanging on to the roof and wherever they could find a hold! When she broke down, some ten miles north of the station, the driver had to cut out one of the horses and ride in for a wagon to fetch the passengers and the luggage and then cripple in with the stage so we could set to work on a repair job."

The man cocked his head in the direction of the smithy and the rhythmic pound of a sledge on heated metal. "By morning we should have that thoroughbrace so it'll hold up the rest of the distance."

"How far is that?" Pryor wanted to know.

"Laredo? Not far. Just shy of thirty miles. That be where you're going?" Seeing the other's nod he frowned slightly as he said, "Funny, I never noticed you ride in. What direction did you come?"

Owen Pryor made a vague gesture, indicating the sun-blistered plains behind him to north and west. "Yonderly."

"By the look of you, you've ridden a piece." Pryor could have said, *Over two hundred and sixty miles in the last four days,* but he merely shrugged.

The station manager continued, "I don't doubt, like all these other pilgrims, you're down to see the hanging." When he got no answer he added, "You sure as hell know about the hanging, don't you? Where've you been? It's Bart Campion—the old curly wolf himself! After all these years, he's actually sitting in the jail at Laredo, tried for murder and convicted and waiting to get strung up!"

Pryor nodded briefly. "Sure, I heard. I thought by now it would likely all be over."

"Not yet. Not till day after tomorrow—at high noon. At least, that's when it's scheduled." The man gave him a knowing look. "But I hear the smart money is betting otherwise. After all, Bart Campion still has a gang, and nobody really thinks they're gonna stand by and let the law string up their boss without them turning a hand! No way of knowing what they might be planning, or when

4

they'll make their move, but every man and his brother has his mind made up to be there when they do.

"It's great for the stage company," he added. "This line's doing business like we never seen before. Running extra coaches and loading them to the axles—doing everything but charge excursion rates. Well, in a couple of days it'll be over and things will all be back to normal."

Owen Pryor was thinking, *So there still may be time!*

All at once the urgency that had been driving him eased a trifle. It left him drained, aware for the first time how close he was to exhaustion. He drew a breath and looked at the blazing sun dropping low toward the flat horizon. Very soon that sun would set and the brief prairie twilight would begin. If he rode on he could still cover some miles before nightfall, but all at once there seemed little to gain by it. The chestnut gelding was as badly used as its rider. There was no sense in pushing themselves until they both dropped.

He asked, "What's the chances of putting up here tonight? I've been on the trail a spell, and me and the horse could use feed."

The man hesitated. "I got no sleeping accommodations. This is only supposed to be a noon stop—the stage would be going on to Laredo tonight if it hadn't broke down. There's a female in the crowd, so I'm letting her have the only bed available. The rest will have to spread blankets where they can. You're welcome to join them. As for grub and grain, I ain't supposed to sell company supplies to anybody but passengers. Still, I guess I can fix you up—say for a couple of dollars."

"Fair enough," Pryor said, and dug two silver cartwheels from his jeans.

Seeing them disappear to the other man's pocket, he had his doubts that the stage line was apt to see any part of

5

that money. "Pick any stall," the man said. "Help yourself to the oat bin. One more thing: I suggest you keep an eye on those pilgrims. The delay has got some of them pretty touchy—they're afraid the fun will all be over before they reach Laredo. One in particular you should watch out for: He's a big, towheaded fellow named Claib Meagher, off the docks at Galveston, and he's just itching to get his hands on a horse. I've already had to refuse to sell him one of these company animals!"

"Thanks for the warning." Pryor took the reins of the weary chestnut. "I'll see that he doesn't get his hands on *this* one."

The station manager left to check the progress of work at the blacksmith shed. The sun was dipping lower now, behind a curtain of blown dust and wavering heat. Pryor, turning to lead his animal toward the low sprawl of the adobe barn, paused a moment as he saw the pair who had just emerged from the station doorway.

There had been mention of a female among the stage passengers; this would have to be the one. She wore a gray traveling dress and jacket that must be almost unbearably warm for this time of year, yet she didn't look at all uncomfortable. The slim young man with her had his coat over his arm, revealing a candy-striped shirt and a shoe-string tie. They stood with their heads together as he pointed out something on the horizon.

The man had straight brown hair; of the woman, Pryor could tell only that she seemed young and shapely. He couldn't see her features clearly, but as he led his horse away he was suddenly conscious of his own unkempt appearance—the sweated shirt, the dusty clothing and untrimmed mustache and shag of unshaven whiskers. A man who lived and worked alone, especially if he seldom had so much as a glimpse of a woman, was very apt to let his appearance go until something called his mind to it.

Molly Bishop noticed the tired-looking man leading his horse to the barn and wondered a little about him—he looked as though he had been riding long and far on urgent business. She thought she could measure his weariness by her own after nearly a week of journeying by stagecoach down the spine of Texas. Days had begun before dawn and ended at dusk—days filled with dust and heat and the unvarying rhythm of hoofbeats and the sway of the coach. Days of drowsing and jostling from the men with whom she found herself surrounded, with their endless talk about the hanging at Laredo to which she had finally tried to shut her ears.

For those men lounging about the station a breakdown and stopover for repairs might be an irritant, but to Molly it was a relief to have solid earth under her feet again. Moreover, it meant she could put off a little longer the decisions that awaited her in Laredo at the end of this journey. She was too confused in her emotions to know if she was glad or sorry for that. Anticipation had become a kind of dread that grew as the miles to Laredo dwindled.

She only half-listened to the young man standing beside her in the station doorway. He called himself Boyce Tuthill and claimed to be a newspaper reporter from Missouri. He showed a natural curiosity about practically everything—he even seemed to find the chaparral of this south Texas country fascinating, different from anything he'd ever seen around his home in Kansas City. Just now he had been quoting from his pocket notebook some of the plant names he'd been collecting from the stage driver, the station agent, and anyone else who would answer his questions: mesquite, salt cedar, huisache . . . he read them off like a litany.

There was an interruption as a couple of stage passengers came out the station door past them. One that Molly had heard identified as a Dallas lawyer was telling the other, "I got twenty dollars says you don't know what the hell you're talking about! Now the law's got him, do you really think they'll let him get away again? You can bet they'll have the army and a company of Texas Rangers on hand, if needed, to see he gets from the jail to the gallows!"

"Make that thirty and you're covered!" said the second man, a pharmacist from Waco. "It ain't some two-bit bankrobber we're talking about. Hell, man! This is Bart Campion!"

They were gone then, taking their endless debate with them, to join a knot of men under the lone live oak. Molly suddenly felt the reporter's hand at her elbow. Boyce Tuthill exclaimed in an anxious voice, "Miss Bishop! You all right?"

She didn't know what he might have read in her face. "Of course."

The young fellow shook his head, showing his concern. "All this talk of hanging!" he exclaimed, in deep disapproval. "I'm sorry you have to listen to it. It's the only thing these men seem to know!"

She managed a smile for him. Boyce Tuthill had been very considerate all during this interminable journey. A sensible young woman, Molly was enough of a realist to know it was probably because she was the only female aboard the overcrowded coach. All the same, the newspaperman did appear to be attracted, and she could scarcely help but respond to that; he had the assertive manner of his breed, but he was fairly good-looking and

8

any woman must at least feel flattered. It was when Boyce Tuthill started to show sympathy that her caution rose like a wall between them.

She was vulnerable and she knew it—lonely, young, without counsel, and bearing an emotional burden that, given half a chance, she would have been more than glad to share with someone. But not Boyce Tuthill! She had to remind herself that a newspaper reporter was the last person in the world she could afford to open her heart to just now.

In the barn Owen Pryor set about caring for his horse—stripping saddle and gear, finding oats and hay for its manger. He was busy with this when he became aware of someone in the barn entrance. He glanced around.

The man who stood watching him was big—taller than Pryor by several inches and constructed on a scale to match. A wild thatch of yellow hair lay along his skull; his brows and whiskers were the same pale color. His eyes were small under a heavy plate of bone, his jaw was solid, and the nose looked as though it might have been broken some time or other—likely in a brawl. His shirt sleeves were rolled up on thick forearms and one of them bore a tattoo in the shape of an anchor.

This, Pryor guessed, would be Claib Meagher, the stevedore off the Galveston docks—he had the look of one.

He said, in a rough growl, "I'm looking at your horse."

"I see you are," Pryor said.

"What's your price for him? Including saddle and gear."

"No price. Sorry."

The pale brows drew down in a scowl. "Hell, everything's got a price! And I ain't exactly a patient man. I want to get movin'! I'm fed up with this place—I'm fed up with cooling my heels while they paste that dumb stagecoach back together!"

"I understand they expect to roll again come daylight," Pryor pointed out. "You should reach Laredo by noon. That's not so bad."

"If you think so," Claib Meagher retorted, "I'll be glad to let you have my seat, and I'll take the horse. I can be there by dawn."

"Not on this horse, you can't. He's had enough for one day. Would you want to run him into the ground?"

The other man shrugged meaty shoulders. "That'll be my problem."

"No it won't. Because I've told you already—I'm not selling."

"Then I just might make you!"

Owen Pryor casually placed his hand on the butt of his holstered gun and let it rest there.

Claib Meagher wasn't wearing a gun; perhaps, in his world of the waterfront, he relied on bluster and on the weight of his fists to get what he wanted. He eyed the smaller man now and his big hand twitched, and angry color began to spread through his cheeks to the edge of his hairline.

"I understand," Pryor said, "you've already been told about staying away from the stage company's horses. That goes for this one, too. I won't warn you again!"

The big fellow's mouth worked and he gave vent to an obscenity. A moment longer his stare held Pryor's. Abruptly he heeled about and went tramping out of the barn, and the sound of his heavy workshoes faded. Owen

Pryor let out a breath. He hadn't been sure the man would back away; he didn't know yet if the warning had really taken. But for the time being he dismissed Claib Meagher from consideration. He had other things on his mind.

He completed his work with the chestnut gelding, finishing by rubbing the animal down with a piece of sacking and checking its hoofs. That done, he opened a pocket of his saddlebags and took out a clean shirt, his razor and soap, and a piece of mirror he carried with him. Having fetched well water, he stripped out of his sweated shirt, washed, and then proceeded to work up a lather and attack the accumulation of stiff black whiskers.

It was refreshing after four hard days of riding the Pecos River and the sun-struck plains of Texas. He told himself that this had nothing at all to do with the pretty woman he had seen in the station doorway. A man had to keep clean, even on a long ride. Yet as he left the barn and crossed to the station building, she wasn't too far from his thoughts.

Smoke rose from the chimney and smells of cooking reached him through the open door and windows. The loiterers had vanished inside and he could hear talk in the station's main room. The young man he'd seen with the girl earlier stood alone now in the doorway smoking a tailor-made cigarette. He nodded to Pryor and announced, "They're just about to serve up. I hope it's going to be better than some of the stage-line food I've been eating!" But then he added, with a close look at the stranger, "I don't remember seeing you on the stage. Maybe you're from around here?"

"Just riding through. Heading for Laredo."

"Boyce Tuthill's the name," the other man said. He had rather sharp but not unpleasant features, and an aggressiveness of manner. Pryor wasn't too surprised when he said, "I'm a newspaperman—from Kansas City, reporter for the *Journal of Commerce*."

"Is that so? Kind of far afield, aren't you?"

"Not at all. I'm after a story—just about the best I ever had a crack at."

Owen Pryor looked at him. "You wouldn't mean the hanging? I'd never have thought Bart Campion would be that much of a drawing card so far away as Missouri."

"Oh, you're dead wrong," the younger man assured him. "Why, if you was to be hanging old Jesse James himself it would hardly make bigger headlines! I expect I won't be the only reporter sent in to cover this story. What I'll be looking for is a fresh angle, one that the rest are apt to miss. Because with luck, I mean to work this into something—maybe even a crack at the St. Louis papers."

Owen Pryor said, a little dryly, "I wouldn't doubt it for a minute!" One thing the man apparently didn't lack was confidence, but he was so open about it that Pryor found himself rather liking him. He said now, "Earlier, I noticed the young lady with you. Your wife?"

"What?" Tuthill looked briefly confused. "I don't have a wife." He added, "You're referring to Miss Bishop—Molly Bishop. She's not with me. She's by herself. Come from someplace east of Dallas, I believe."

"All by herself? Isn't this a pretty rough crowd for her?"

"I agree." Tuthill looked definitely concerned. "She strikes me as awfully young for traveling alone, though she seems able enough to take care of herself. But I've tried to look out for her—helped her find a seat by the window, stayed close as I could in case I'm needed. For whatever reason she seems determined about making this journey, though she hasn't volunteered any information

12

about herself. Of course," he added quickly, "it really isn't any of my business. All the same—"

He broke off. He had seen something through the door of the station that caused him to stiffen, and then the young man gave an exclamation, flung aside the cigarette he had been smoking, and started through the door. Curious, Owen Pryor moved to follow.

The stage station's main room was long and low-ceilinged; its thick mud walls kept it reasonably cool. Much of the space was filled by a long trestle table, where the stage passengers had their meals. This table was set now with china plates and cheap silverware, and some of the men from the stage were already seated; they were all watching the curtained doorway at the far end that evidently led to the kitchen and sleeping quarters. Pryor saw that the young woman, Molly Bishop, had come out. Apparently she had volunteered to help get the food on the table, for she carried a bowl of potatoes cooked with their jackets on and a steaming pot of coffee.

But she had found her way blocked by Claib Meagher. The towhead towered over her. He had a whiskey bottle, and it looked as though he had been helping himself to its contents. As Pryor watched, the young woman tried to step to one side but Meagher moved with her, deliberately blocking the way. She halted, frowning, encumbered by the food in her hands and perhaps a little frightened. Throughout the room the men from the stage watched silently; nobody looked in a mood to interfere.

Claib Meagher said loudly, "You been too stuck up to give me so much as the time of day! I suppose you think I ain't good enough! Well, this time you ain't gonna breeze past me with your nose in the air. I think you're gonna say, 'How about a little kiss, Mister Meagher?'

And after that you're gonna say, 'Thank *you,* Mister Meagher!' You understand me?"

Someone snickered. The girl's face, just visible past the man's broad shoulder, was pale despite the heat of the kitchen she had just left, but she stood her ground. Steam curled upward from the dish she was holding. She didn't look to any of the other men for help—perhaps she sensed that they were all with Meagher, or not about to risk interfering. Her mouth was tight and her voice trembled a little as she told him, "I'd hate to waste perfectly good food, but if you don't leave me alone you're going to get this bowl of potatoes right in your face!"

Owen Pryor felt like saying *Bravo!* Claib Meagher swore and laid a hand on the girl's wrist, as though thinking she might actually carry out her threat. By that time the reporter, young Boyce Tuthill, was already making his way across the room and skirting the big table. He seized the big man by a shoulder. "Take your hands off her!" he exclaimed. "Leave her alone!"

He was a full head short of Meagher's height and dwarfed by the man's bulk. But, taken by surprise, Meagher was thrown off balance and the whiskey bottle shot out of his hand, to hit the adobe wall with a smash. He whirled about, the girl momentarily forgotten. He cursed, and the back of one heavy fist cuffed Tuthill across the face.

The smaller man was flung backward to fall against the table and the men seated there leaped to their feet, yelling. Meagher started for the newspaperman as he lay dazed and sprawled upon the hard-packed dirt floor. It looked to Pryor that if he wasn't prevented, he was just drunkenly furious enough to stomp the man under his heavy work shoes.

A shout from Pryor failed to halt Meagher. Then

14

Pryor drew his gun as he waded forward, shoving one of the yelling stage passengers out of the way. The roar of the gun, within the room's confining walls, silenced the yelling voices. Everything froze, and even Claib Meagher stood motionless while adobe dust, kicked loose by the bullet that stamped into the low roof above his head, drifted down in a gray fog about him.

Pryor reached the man, placed the muzzle of the smoking gun against the bully's thick chest, and drove him back from the one he had meant to stomp. "No you don't!" he said crisply.

Meagher stood pinned by the gun barrel, his big hands hanging empty at his sides as his stare met Pryor's. The reek of whiskey on his breath mingled with the smells of burnt powder, of spilled food and drifting dust. Now there was a sound of running footsteps and the station agent came bursting in from outside with a burly man close at his heels that Pryor took to be the stage driver. The bald-headed agent demanded, "What the hell's going *on?*"

Pryor holstered his gun. "This fellow insulted the girl," he said. "Sorry for the gunplay."

"No need to apologize for that!" the man replied gruffly; and the stage driver added, "I pegged that guy for a troublemaker the minute he clumb aboard my coach."

Meagher had turned belligerent. He told Owen Pryor, "I'd like to see you lay aside that gun!"

Pryor answered coldly, "When the stage gets in at Laredo tomorrow, I mean to check up on how you behaved yourself. If I find you bothered this lady again, I'll be looking for you!"

The driver said gruffly, "Don't worry. If he acts up I'll kick him off the stage and let him walk the rest of the way! That's a promise!"

Claib Meagher swung his head like a baited bull. He muttered an obscenity and suddenly turned and went striding out of the room, bulling someone out of his path. The station agent said quickly, "I better make sure he doesn't try for one of those horses!" He followed the big man out as the room broke into a babble of talk. Owen Pryor decided the incident was over.

He looked at Boyce Tuthill and saw the young fellow sitting up, shaking his head groggily. His nose was bleeding. He shrugged aside the hand Pryor offered, saying, "I can manage." Instead he grabbed hold of the table and hauled himself to his feet.

"Are you all right?" Pryor insisted.

He merely got a cold stare as the other man dug into a pocket and brought out a handkerchief to stem the bleeding. Owen Pryor ignored his hostility—it was a matter of pride. It was only natural that he resented someone having to step in after he failed to stand up to Claib Meagher.

Molly Bishop hadn't moved from where she stood. Her face was ashen. She still held the serving bowl and the heavy coffeepot, and Pryor said gruffly, "Here! Let me have those!" Moving to take them he got his first good look at her and was surprised to discover how young she seemed to be—she could hardly be twenty. Her eyes were brown, her lips full—a strikingly handsome girl. She said nothing, but her look, meeting his, held gratitude and something else that could only be warm admiration. He turned from her with a feeling of embarrassment.

Setting his burdens on the table, he again caught Boyce Tuthill's stare and this time he read it right. There was more here than damaged pride and resentment. The young fellow had seen Molly Bishop's expression, and his own was plainly filled with simple jealousy.

16

Chapter 2

That meal was a strange one. At the end of the long table where Molly Bishop sat with Pryor and Tuthill there was almost no conversation. The girl was silent, perhaps in reaction to the ordeal with Claib Meagher. Young Tuthill tried to draw her out, but with little success, and Pryor spoke seldom. Once, in answer to a direct question, he admitted to being a cattle rancher. "At least," he said, "I've got a little place over in New Mexico that has about enough grass for a handful of steers to make some kind of living." He offered no explanation as to what had placed him here on the road to Laredo, and he wasn't asked.

Claib Meagher, having tramped back into the station, had taken over the far end of the table and held it in a sullen silence of his own, shoveling food away and sending his malevolent stare up the length of the table at Molly Bishop and her champions. But the rest of the crowd was noisy enough, especially when the stage driver stuck his head in the door to announce that repairs to the thoroughbrace had been completed. The coach was in running order and would be rolling at daylight on the last leg of its interrupted run to Laredo.

That news galvanized the crowd of men around the table and they erupted in a hot debate over the one topic that was uppermost with all of them—the public hanging at Laredo two days hence at high noon; or, to be more exact, the hanging that most of them seemed sure would never take place. When Owen Pryor got up from the table, the crowd was arguing whether Bart Campion's followers would make a daylight raid on the jail building or try to break him out of his cell at night. Or would they boldly pluck him from the steps of the gallows itself? The general worry was that, because of the mishap to the stage, it would all happen before they could be on hand to see the fun.

Pryor left, disgusted at their wrangling, and went out to the barn to check on his horse.

All seemed to be well. Afterward he paused in the doorway to roll up a cigarette and get it going, enjoying the first drag of smoke into his lungs. The sun had finally set. The big coach stood in silhouette against the fading smear of color along the flat horizon; Pryor walked over for a look at it and at the repair job that had been done. The broken stanchion had been crudely but effectively replaced, the thick leather thoroughbrace was once more intact. With luck the coach was in shape to complete its run tomorrow.

He was turning toward the station building when he saw a lone figure standing out there in the stage road that ran into the distance through this desolate emptiness of mesquite and sage and prickly pear. It was Molly Bishop, and on an impulse he went to her, seeing her wary lift of head and then her quick smile when she recognized him.

"Going for a stroll after supper?" he said. "You're wise to stay on the road—it might not be safe wandering off of it: too many rattlesnakes. Do you mind if I walk along with you a bit?"

"No, I'd like that," she said, and he fell in beside her.

The thought of snakes didn't seem to disturb her. What she really wanted, he suspected, was a chance to get clear away from that noisy crowd at the station for a few minutes at least—to be alone where it was quiet and she didn't have to be aware of their eyes constantly upon her. She walked slowly, her head lifted, her hands behind her back, and Pryor adjusted his pace to hers. Eyes closed, she drew in deeply of the air that held the scent of heated dust and miles of thorny chaparral. She said, "I've lived all my life in Texas, but I never realized till now just how big it is."

"It's that, all right," he agreed.

She turned to him suddenly. "I haven't thanked you properly. That awful man! I was terrified—and all the rest simply looked on!"

"All but Boyce Tuthill," he reminded her. "I wouldn't have stepped in, except I saw that he'd run into a little more trouble than he could handle."

"I was terribly sorry that he got hurt!"

Pryor said sternly, "You'll pardon my saying it, but I'm afraid you're only asking for such trouble by traveling alone in company like that. I can't believe that you're even twenty-one yet."

She admitted it, after the briefest pause: "I'm eighteen. . . . I know what I'm doing isn't very smart—but I simply have to make this journey."

"There's no one who could have come with you? Or refused to let you come alone?"

"There's no one at all. . . ."

She had halted, and he saw her clutch both elbows with a visible shudder. Though the sun had set and the brief dusk had begun, the baked earth was still giving back the day's long heat. Pryor said, frowning, "You aren't cold, are you?"

"Oh, no," she said in a small voice. "Frightened, I guess. It must be a reaction to what almost happened in there." And then, as he stood beside her, helpless to know what he could do or say that might comfort this strange girl, she suddenly lifted her eyes to him and said, "Mister Pryor, just how much do you know about—about this man they're going to hang day after tomorrow?"

The question caught him off guard. He looked at her sharply. "Bart Campion? Why, what anyone else would know, I suppose. That he's been an outlaw a long time— at first, against the carpetbaggers, starting ten years ago after the war ended. That's always made him and the gang he headed seem pretty much like heroes to a lot of people in this part of the world. A myth like that is hard to kill, though I'm afraid it wasn't long before he forgot all about the carpetbaggers and began stealing from other Texans. In the eyes of the law, I'm afraid by now he's no better than an ordinary criminal."

"But it was my understanding that he's to be hanged for—" Her voice faltered over the word. "For murder . . ."

"That's so. His gang has chalked up some killings through the years; up to now, as far as anybody knows, he's kept his own hands clean. But the story is that he had a personal enemy down there in Laredo—a sheriff named Donnelly that he held some grudge against. A few weeks ago, from what I heard, he rode in and shot the man in front of witnesses. He was grabbed and put on trial, and it was a foregone conclusion what the verdict would be. . . ." As he was talking, Molly Bishop had dropped her eyes, but he could see the look on her face and he broke off to exclaim, "Molly! Is something wrong?"

Her fingers were twisted tightly together. She said on a note of anguish, "I suppose anyone would say, after what you've told me, that I've made a terrible mistake. But going to Laredo was something I *had* to do. I still have to!"

He stared, uncomprehending. "Are you trying to tell me you have something to do with Bart Campion?"

"I've got to see him. I've got to talk to him before it's too late!"

"Campion? *Why?*"

She hesitated, then blurted it out, as though under pressure to unload a burden she had carried too far alone. "I have to know from him if it's possible that—that he could be my father!"

The first stirring of a night breeze, still freighted with the dusty heat of the Texas plains, gusted at them as they stood there in the wheel tracks of the stage road. It rattled the dry brush and brought them the sound of a burst of laughter from the men in the stage station yonder. It tugged at the ends of the girl's brown hair and she put up a hand to capture them—an instinctive and feminine gesture.

"You think this is some crazy notion of mine," she said, a trifle stiffly. "But let me explain: Since my mother died two years ago I've been on my own. Most of that time I was working in a small boardinghouse—so, I guess you can see I'm not completely inexperienced with men like Claib Meagher! I have no living relatives. I can hardly even remember my—" She corrected herself. "I don't really remember Tom Bishop, the man whose name I carry; I was only about three years old when he went off to the war, and he never came back.

"I'm certain about one thing: Sometime before she married—long before the carpetbaggers made him an outlaw, Bart Campion had some part in my mother's life. She was a young girl living on the farm, over in east Texas. He was young then, too, of course. I don't know just what their relationship amounted to, or how long it lasted. But as the years passed she spoke of him often. And though I could never bring myself to ask directly, there were many, many hints she let drop that convinced me she was suggesting things she wouldn't actually say."

Listening to this, Owen Pryor was aware of the slow crawling of an emotion that was something very like cold horror. It was a struggle finding words to say to this girl, but some instinct warned him that he must treat the matter with complete seriousness. He was studying her face more carefully as he asked suddenly, "Have you ever seen a picture of Bart Campion? To look for any trace of resemblance?"

She shook her head. "I doubt if it would prove anything. I've always looked just like my mother."

"And supposing this thing turned out to be true? What then? Would you feel proud of the fact—or ashamed?" He spoke more bluntly than he intended, but she didn't seem to take offense.

"Pride or shame has nothing to do with it," the girl insisted. "Can't you understand? The way it is, I don't even know who I *am!* Surely everybody has a right to know—but all I ever had was a question mark that's shadowed my whole life. And not until now did I suppose there was any chance I might someday meet my real father, face to face, and find out the truth.

"So that's why I'm here," she finished, and her jaw set stubbornly. "Even if you think it's the most foolish thing in the world!"

There was no way to argue with such determination; still, Owen Pryor could do no less than try. "If you're asking my opinion," he said carefully, "then, yes—I can't help thinking it was a mistake to come. Laredo is about the worst place in the world, just now, for a young girl alone. The whole town will be worked up and full of men like those pilgrims on the stage—and what makes you suppose that the ones who are holding Bart Campion will want to bother with you or let you anywhere near him?"

She looked down at the toe of her shoe as she worked at the dirt with it. She said in a small voice, "Of course I've thought of that."

"But then, let's say you do manage to see him," Pryor went on insistently. "Let's say that it turns out he *is* your father, and you still find some trace in him of the man your mother was once attracted to. How in the world will you be able to face it then—knowing what's going to happen to him?"

It was a long moment before she spoke again, and then it was to ask slowly, "What those men on the stage are saying—do you think there could be any truth in it?"

"About Campion's gang trying a rescue?"

She nodded. Pryor frowned as, almost unbidden, a succession of remembered faces passed through his mind: Duke Ridge, Merl Loomis, Red Banning . . . But, no—he corrected himself—the newspapers had said Banning got himself killed at Waco, in '73. That was in the raid on the express office when Jim Dance, too, was seriously wounded by a load of buckshot. No way of knowing how many others would have fallen away during the years by a

23

natural process of attrition, or how many new faces had been recruited to fill out the ranks. As long as Bart Campion stood at their head, the force of his leadership would keep it always the same gang though some of its members changed. But what had happened now the gang was left on its own?

Owen Pryor demanded bluntly, "What do you want me to say—that you have nothing to worry about? That your . . . father's friends—if he is your father—will be able to save him in the nick of time?" He shook his head. "I'm afraid you've asked me a question I can't answer."

"I see. . . ."

Molly Bishop swung away from him suddenly, saying in a lifeless voice, "I guess I don't want to walk any more. I'm tireder than I thought, and they say we're to get an early start tomorrow." She faced him long enough to add, "Good evening, Mister Pryor. Thank you for answering honestly."

She started away for the station building, where Boyce Tuthill, a dimly seen figure in his striped shirt, stood in the dusk watching them. Looking after her and thinking of those last words, Pryor could only remind himself of all the things he might have told her, had he been really honest, about the man she believed to be her father.

Having scouted the ground for scorpions or a possible rattlesnake, Pryor spread his blankets near enough to the barn that he would be roused if Claib Meagher or anyone else had further designs on the chestnut. But he slept undisturbed and by gray morning was up and ready to ride long before those at the station even began to stir. He left without breakfast. With four days behind him and thirty miles to go, impatience was stronger than the lingering saddle-weariness. He was already a good piece along the south road before dawn broke over the brush-strewn land in an explosion of light and furnace heat.

Chapter 3

From a few miles' distance, where the access road branched off from the stage trace, the ranch headquarters had looked promising, but when Pryor came nearer he saw he had been fooled. The adobe buildings and mesquite-pole corrals were deserted, already on the verge of tumbling down and mingling again with the hardpan and chaparral. The vegas were giving way to catclaw and prickly pear.

It was sight of the well that had lured him off his course, but when he dismounted and tossed a pebble into it, he listened in vain for an answering splash. He nodded bleakly to himself. Dry! That explained why this jacal had been deserted and left to retreat again into the chaparral—if your water source failed you, there was nothing else for it! Pryor slapped the chestnut on its sweaty, dusty shoulder and said, "Too bad. You're thirstier than I am, but there's nothing we can do about it here. Shouldn't be much more than an hour from where we're going. We can tough it out, I guess."

He lingered a moment from curiosity to poke around the adobe house. The slab door, on rotten leather hinges, sagged and had to be pushed open across the hard-packed dirt floor. There was a single room, a couple of windows.

Nothing in the way of furniture had been left behind except a table with a broken leg.

Pryor drew the door shut behind him as he went back outside and returned to mount his horse. With the instinct of a man who knew the value of improvisation, he committed the location of the starved-out, dried-out ranch headquarters to memory as he sent the chestnut again toward the stage road.

With the sun standing at noon in a brassy sky, he approached at last the end of the trail that had stretched over nearly three hundred miles and days of hard riding. It was with mixed emotions that he entered this town of Laredo—a place he once had never expected to see again.

For over two centuries the old pueblo had stood here in the river's sharp bend. It had been built at the chief lower crossing of the Rio Bravo—which gringos called the Rio Grande—at a time when Texas was part of Mexico. It could hardly have changed since he last saw it: a dusty spread of streets and adobe buildings, its life slow-paced in the river's muggy heat. A short distance west of town the scattered buildings of a military base, Fort McIntosh, shimmered in the heat haze. All in all, it seemed a place where nothing ever would change.

But now as he moved deeper into the heart of the pueblo, Pryor became aware of the number of men he saw and the volume of noise they made. They seemed to be everywhere—in the rutted streets, under the shade of brush-and-viga arcades, passing along the hard-packed pathways and in and out of saloons and eating places and cantinas. Voices tumbled through the wide-open and shadowed doorways—a hubbub of sound with an under-current of tension and excitement working through it.

He became aware of a stuttering pound of hammers,

27

and then the sprawl of the courthouse came into sight and he saw at once what the sound meant. He drew rein under a tall cottonwood with a hot wind ripping through its branches above his head. Here there was a water trough, and he let the chestnut sink its muzzle into the leaf-strewn surface while he watched the gallows going up yonder on the courthouse lawn. It was nearly finished. The clean white timbers of new pine made a dazzle in the sunlight and gave off a smell of pitch. Mexican workmen, up on the raised platform, were just now hoisting the high crossbar into place and driving home the heavy square nails to hold it. Watching in silence were more of the crowd that had come flocking to the ancient pueblo.

Pryor took his grim stare from the raw lumber and skeleton frame of the gallows and put it instead on the onlookers, wondering at the nature of man and of these men in particular.

Like those on the stagecoach, they ran to no particular type. He saw sun-browned men with the look of farmers or cowboys, others who might be laborers or shopkeepers or their assistants; perhaps a blacksmith and a lawyer, and one who might even be a schoolteacher. Another, a potbellied fellow, looked prosperous enough to be a banker. There were even a few women, including one or two who were well dressed and carried parasols against the power of the noon sun.

To Owen Pryor, the whole thing had a ghoulish aspect. Yet life on the frontier was hard and often humdrum, and any rare break in its routine came as something to be seized on. Adding to that the notoriety of the prisoner in the Laredo jail, the presence of a crowd was hardly to be wondered at.

The chestnut finished drinking and tossed its head. Pryor settled it, then turned his attention to the jail.

It was a small stone building that sat by itself to the rear of the courthouse. Recollection darkened his stare and drew out the line of his mouth as he looked at it. How long had it been? Five years since he spent almost a month in that jail behind those same barred windows! It seemed half a lifetime ago. Remembering how young he'd been then, he now felt ancient. The emotions that filled him turned him suddenly restless. He gave a muttered exclamation and reined away. But dark thoughts rode with him as he left that place behind and rode on through the dusty town, making for the ferry slip at the foot of Convent Avenue.

Where the bluff on which the pueblo sat broke away, the Rio Grande slid by with Nuevo Laredo on the farther bank. The ferry was just pulling in. He dismounted to watch it unload a Mexican family, a couple of Anglo cowhands, and an ancient with skin the color of leather, whose shoulders bent under the weight of a crate of chickens as he hoisted it to his back and tottered away up the hill. When the clumsy craft had emptied, Pryor paid his fee and led the chestnut gelding aboard. He was the only Mexico-bound passenger. Standing in the bow, smelling the dark scent of the river, he squinted at the sun smear on sliding brown water that reflected heat into his face as the opposite bank drew nearer. There he mounted again and rode up the hill into Laredo's counterpart in the Mexican state of Tamaulipas.

He could have stepped into another century. In five years, things had changed little north of the river, but here in Old Mexico one had the feeling of a completely timeless land. When he tied his horse in front of a certain cantina and stepped inside, he was almost surprised not to see faces from the past waiting for him. But the place was empty except for a couple of natives and, alone in a corner, a man with the look of an Americano who favored Pryor with a keen and searching glance. Pryor ordered a beer and plate of beans and tortillas. The beer was warm; as he waited for his food he sipped at it and looked again at that corner table. The man was staring at him. Reluctantly he turned and walked over there, carrying the beer. He said shortly, "You know me, Bill?"

"It took me a minute. You've changed some."

"You haven't, much."

Bill Longley toyed with the glass of tequila he had in front of him. He was a man about Pryor's age, perhaps in his mid-twenties, a big fellow, two hundred pounds on a six-foot frame that made him look leaner than that. His broad shoulders were slightly stooped. His hair and curled mustache and imperial goatee were black, but what you noticed were the piercing eyes beneath heavy brows.

There was no more notorious killer in the entire Southwest. Pryor didn't suppose anyone knew how many dead men Bill Longley had left behind him on an erratic trail that stretched across Texas and as far afield as Salt Lake City. Thirty at least, it was said. At the age of sixteen he'd ridden and killed with Cullen Baker's cutthroat outfit but had gone far beyond them, a lone wolf by nature. He killed with little need for an excuse; a good number of his victims had been black, simply because Wild Bill Longley hated the color of their skins and the fact that the war had set them free. Owen Pryor looked at him now with cold distaste, but he knew the man to be thoroughly dangerous—someone to be treated with caution.

The sharp black eyes returned his stare. "I don't seem able to lay hold to your name right off," Bill Longley said. "But maybe I never knew it. Seems to me there was something you used to call yourself. Something dumb and fancy . . . The Salado Kid—wasn't that it?" And he repeated it, with a look of amusement that caused Pryor's cheeks to grow warm.

"All right!" Pryor replied, a little too sharply. "I was a lot younger and I fancied how it sounded."

Bill Longley made wet circles on the table with the bottom of his glass as he narrowly considered the other man. "Had anyone asked, I'd have said you were still in Huntsville."

"Time passes," Owen Pryor said with a shrug. "I've been out a couple of years."

"For a fact? Strange—I hadn't heard of it."

It seemed to bother Longley. There was an astonishingly efficient grapevine that let the members of the long-riding community keep informed of everything that went on among their kind. Longley would be wondering why it had failed him in this instance. Owen Pryor explained: "Since I got out of prison, I haven't been anyplace or done anything you were apt to have heard of. I've kept clean, working cattle and staying clear away from Texas."

"Oh?" Longley's cold stare passed over the other man's well-worn, almost shabby clothing. He said in a dry tone, "I wouldn't say you were getting rich at it."

"That's all right. At least I generally know where my next meal is coming from. I sleep pretty good. And I don't have to look over my shoulder!"

The gunman thought that over. "Every man to his own poison," he agreed indifferently. "But it makes me wonder what you're doing here at Laredo. I don't suppose you'd be interested in the hanging tomorrow. If there *is* one," he added with a cold grin.

"*If* there is?" Pryor caught up on that instantly. Without waiting for an invitation he pulled out a chair for himself, dropped his hat on the floor beside his dusty boots, and studied the sardonic features across the table from him. "You think there might not be?" he prompted. "Do you know something—or have you just heard a rumor?"

"Oh, there's no shortage of rumors," the other assured him. "They're all over the place—and if they should turn out to be right I don't intend to miss the fun! Things are a little warm for me in Texas just now—but if anything should develop, I'm close enough here I can ease across the river long enough to watch what happens."

It could hardly make any difference to a man like Bill Longley whether Bart Campion mounted the gallows at noon tomorrow or not. On the other hand, a rescue attempt would strike him as an interesting spectacle, whatever came of it.

Pryor said, "If everyone else has heard these rumors, it stands to reason the authorities are alerted, too."

"You mean Harry Swain? Oh, he's heard, all right."

"Swain!" Pryor stared. "Is *he* still around?"

"Didn't you know? He was Ed Donnelly's undersheriff; now, with his boss dead, he's in charge. It's the biggest thing that ever came his way. He was the one that captured Bart. He strutted all through the trial, and he's been stalling the execution so he can get every scrap of publicity out of it. Trouble is, he's overdone things. All at once the rumors have him scared.

"He's called on the Rangers for help, but they got their hands full elsewhere, and I hear the colonel over at Fort McIntosh is completely fed up with Swain's bragging—says it's a mess the civilians have cooked up for themselves, and he'll have no part in it. What's more, he's declared the town off limits for his troops during the next forty-eight hours to keep them from drinkin' and fightin' with the crowd. So, if Harry finds himself in trouble tomorrow, he's got nobody but himself to thank for it, or look to for help."

The dark stare narrowed on Pryor. "But why all the questions, since you say it's no concern of yours anymore? I've even forgotten: Just how long was it you rode with Campion?"

"Less than a year," Pryor said. "Actually I went on just one job with the gang—that was the bank at Eagle Pass—and then I only went along to hold the horses. A couple of weeks later we stopped off here in Nuevo Laredo—this very cantina. I wasn't known hereabouts so Bart sent me across to scout on the American side of the river and see how things looked for a job. But someone spotted me who had been at Eagle Pass. He tipped off the sheriff and the next thing I knew I was in jail, waiting to be shipped back there for trial. Three years in Huntsville Prison, and I've never laid eyes on any of the Campion gang since."

"Luck of the draw, Kid," Longley said with a shrug.

"It was probably the luckiest thing that could have happened," Pryor retorted. "I was young and I was a damn fool. At least I found that out before it was too late."

Bill Longley drained off his glass and, setting it down, made a face over the fiery liquor. Chair legs screeched as he got to his feet. "If that's your idea of good luck," he said dryly, "maybe I better get away from you before some of it rubs off on me!" But he paused a moment—a solid figure, holstered gun riding heavy on one hip. He said, "I might tell you, I saw a couple of Campion's boys last night standing at the bar. Duke Ridge and Merl Loomis. We didn't talk," he added. "I never had much use for either of them. I thought you might be interested."

Pryor could not deny the sudden speeding of his pulse, knowing then that all the rumors were true. He tried to keep his tone casual as he suggested, "I don't suppose you would have seen or heard anything about another one of the gang—a fellow named Jim Dance?"

Longley repeated the name, stroking the short black imperial. He shook his head. "I know the one you mean. No, I haven't seen him; but if the rest of Campion's boys are in the neighborhood, it's likely he would be, too. If I run into him, I'll tell him you were asking."

Pryor nodded. "Do that." The gunman left at a lithe and easy prowl, checking the noisy street before he stepped from the doorway into the dazzling heat of high noon.

Just then the man came with the food Pryor had ordered. It was burning stuff, well laced with the hottest Mexican seasoning; but he was suddenly ravenous, too hungry to mind as he tore into it.

Chapter 4

From the start Claib Meagher and a few chosen cronies had appropriated the swaying roof of the stagecoach, preferring to cling there in the direct heat of the sun rather than cram themselves into the inside seats. Molly could hear them up there, shouting and laughing over an inexhaustible store of dirty stories, an occasional freak current of heated air bringing tobacco smoke swirling in with the wind and dust that came blindingly through the open windows.

By contrast, those inside seemed too worn down by fatigue to have energy for conversation; or perhaps they were simply talked out. They stared silently at one another or at the blur of flat and unchanging landscape. With the removable center seat in place, allowing three additional passengers to be crowded into the coach, there was scarcely room for a person's knees; they had been traveling like this, cramped for space, since leaving Dallas. All a person could do, if he was lucky enough to manage a seat by the window, was hold on to the tug strap and endure this interminable journey. And hope that there would be no further breakdowns or mishaps.

Molly was constantly aware of Boyce Tuthill seated next to her—always there at her elbow, always ready with a steadying hand if a chuckhole or a swerve of the horses caused the swaying coach to throw her off balance. She was grateful for the kindness he had shown her, but she seemed unable to enter into his attempts at conversation. Her mind was too full of turmoil and uncertainty over what she would find waiting at journey's end.

More than once she found her thoughts turning to that strange man at the stage station—the one who called himself Owen Pryor—who had put Claib Meagher in his place and afterward walked with her in the dusk. It rather astonished her to recall she had opened up and told this man things she had never discussed before with any other person. There must have been a need, greater even than she had realized, to bring out into the open the gnawing questions about her identity—to share them and hear someone's opinion and advice. But why Owen Pryor, rather than a person like, for instance, Boyce Tuthill?

She didn't know. That troubled her, especially as she recalled that there had been something almost forbidding in Pryor's face, something she could in no way interpret, when she spoke of Bart Campion.

That conversation in the dusk, she felt certain, was one she would long remember.

She must have slept, finally, under the monotony and the swaying of the coach and the hum of iron-tired wheels and steady plod of hoofs. A sound of voices around her stirred her awake, and then Boyce Tuthill spoke beside her saying, "We're coming in. This must be Laredo!"

She stirred herself and straightened, for the moment completely confused and disoriented. Everyone around her was excited; on the roof men were shouting. She had a glimpse of a few scattered adobe buildings huddled in a mist of heat haze. And then the twin ruts of the stage road became a dusty street, with houses and vacant lots on either hand.

Boyce Tuthill asked, "Do you have someone to meet you?"

She shook her head. "I don't know a soul here in Laredo."

"You don't?" He didn't seem able to believe his ears. "Then just where do you expect to stay?"

"I really hadn't thought. I'll have to look for a place. A room of some kind."

"In *this* town? Right now?" The young man could only stare at her. "Whatever there might be in the way of a hotel, or boardinghouses, they're bound to be crowded to overflowing."

He was right, of course. She should have realized as much herself. She said nothing as she considered the problem.

They were well into the town now. A dog ran alongside, barking at the horses. Men were leaning out the coach windows yelling, and on the street other people shouted back. All at once, without any preliminary slowing of speed, the driver hauled in on his leathers and tromped his brake, and as the teams dropped to their haunches the big coach rocked violently on its thorough-braces and the dust billowed around it. The door flew open, passengers burst out, and those on the roof began scrambling to the ground.

"This is the station. Be a good idea if you stay close to me," Boyce Tuthill suggested. He moved the center seat out of the way, climbed out himself, and then turned to give Molly a hand down the high iron step. Afterward he kept hold of her hand and led her out of the confused press of people around the coach.

In scant shade at one corner of the adobe station was a wooden table and bench. Tuthill told Molly, "Stay here while I collect our luggage, and I'll ask around and see what I can find out for you."

She looked into his earnest, serious face. His upper lip was still swollen where big Claib Meagher's backhanded blow had struck; noticing that, she felt sudden concern for him and she said apologetically, "I'm afraid I've been a lot of trouble."

"Not at all!" he said quickly. "Just wait here," he repeated and left her.

She placed her handbag on the table while she stood and looked around her.

For a moment the screen of the crowd seemed to shift apart and she found herself facing Claib Meagher. As their eyes met Molly stiffened, steeling herself for another confrontation. But if that was what he intended he seemed to change his mind. His pale brows drew down into a scowl and he turned his head and spat into the dirt. Then he swung his big frame around and went tramping off as someone moved in between, and the forward set of the big man's head and the meaty thrust of his shoulders were lost to her sight. Molly made herself relax. Perhaps the man had learned his lesson. More likely, now that he had reached Laredo he had more important things on his mind.

Suddenly she found herself remembering that final warning Meagher had received from Owen Pryor yesterday—that Pryor would be checking up on him, to see how he'd behaved himself during the balance of this stage trip. She scanned the crowd and admitted to a feeling of disappointment when she failed to see Pryor among them. But of course she hadn't really expected to. He had only been giving a pointed reminder to the big man to watch

38

his step. There was no reason to think he'd really meant to follow up on it by being on hand when the stage rolled in.

Presently Molly saw Boyce Tuthill returning, carrying her suitcase and his own. He set them down and took out his handkerchief; removing his bowler hat he mopped sweat from his forehead while he made his report. "The town's really bursting at the seams. Every hotel room is already taken—some sleeping two and three strangers to a bed, and all of them here for only one reason. After the doings tomorrow, of course, it'll soon empty out again, but meanwhile it's a real question what we're going to do with *you!*"

"I'm terribly sorry!" When she saw how hard he was taking the situation, Molly had to swallow her own discouragement and force a smile. "It isn't your fault!" she said quickly. "It's mine—I should have stopped to think that it might be like this. But please don't worry. I'll be all right."

He went right on as though she hadn't spoken. "I did hear of one possibility. I understand there's a man and his wife, name of Jackson, who have a grocery store over on San Bernardo Street. The person who mentioned them said he knows for certain they have an extra bedroom in their house that's not being used. I think it's worth looking into. Let's see if we can't talk these people into letting you have it."

"Oh, I don't think so. Surely, if they were of a mind to, they must have had every opportunity to rent it these last few days. So there must be some good reason why they didn't."

"No matter!" Tuthill said bluntly. "Somewhere we've got to find a place for you. The Jacksons may not know it yet, but I have an idea they're going to end up by offering you one. Now, don't argue with me, Molly!" He picked up both their bags, his manner determined. "Come along!"

For just a moment she had a resentful feeling that he was trying to bully her. But she supposed he had good cause to be put out with her for the way she had mismanaged her affairs. There was no question that he had her interests at heart and she was grateful; seeing no alternative she quickly fell in step, clutching her handbag as she let him lead her through the dusty, crowded streets.

He wasted no time—apparently he had already asked full directions to the place he was looking for. This was plainly a very old town, and time could have changed it little. But if there was beauty in the ancient pueblo, with its baked-mud houses and dusty trees, Molly was unable to see much of it in her uncertainty and fatigue. Boisterous throngs seemed to have taken over the narrow streets. Once, as they were passing a saloon, there was a sudden eruption through the open doorway—angry men bursting out, urging on a pair who were locked in combat. Fists flew, blows landed, dust rose as the fighting spilled across the street and became general.

Boyce Tuthill drew Molly hastily out of danger and shoved one of the bags under his arm, freeing a hand. He took hold of her and said, "Quick! This way!" as he almost hauled her across the street to the farther side. He hustled her on until the brawling had been left behind and she was allowed to stop and catch her breath.

Tuthill looked flushed and angry, perhaps a little frightened. "I almost walked you into that!" he exclaimed hoarsely. "I'm sorry! The mood this town is in just now . . . the amount of liquor that's being drunk . . . I guess a person can't be too careful!"

Molly tried to give him a reassuring smile. "It's nothing you could help." She put up a shaky hand to push at her hair, which seemed on the verge of coming down; she felt sweaty and flustered and very unattractive. She told him, with sincere appreciation, "It just makes me realize how lucky I am, having someone go to this much trouble to help me."

"My pleasure," he assured her. "I think the shop we're looking for should be around this next corner. . . ."

The grocery was a small adobe building, set cheek-by-jowl with others, its interior a neat clutter of foodstuffs in bins and barrels and on shelves. At Tuthill's suggestion Molly stayed by the door while he approached the counter; as he did so a woman came through a storeroom entrance at the rear. She was tiny, with birdlike and wrinkled features, thinning gray hair done up in a neat bun, and bright blue eyes behind rimless spectacles. Tuthill set down his burdens and they stood at the counter talking while Molly waited a trifle uncomfortably, unable to make out what they were saying, but aware of glances the woman gave her. Presently the young man turned and beckoned for her to join them.

"Mrs. Jackson," he said, "this is Molly Bishop. I know she'll appreciate anything you can do."

The bright eyes were turned full on Molly. The little woman had to tilt her head slightly to look up at her. Molly, about to offer some routine phrase of greeting, was silenced as she saw the real concern in the older woman's eyes. "Oh, my dear!" Mrs. Jackson exclaimed. Quickly she came around from behind the counter and seized one of Molly's hands in both of hers, which were frail things of bone and soft flesh and thick blue veins. "But of course we'll have to do something!" She turned and called into the storeroom. "Will, come out here! There's someone I want you to meet."

A stoop-shouldered old man, not much taller than

his wife, shuffled in from the back room. He blinked uncertainly from one to another until his wife placed a hand on his arm and turned him toward Molly. "Will, this young lady just got off the stage and she needs a place to stay while she's in Laredo. You know how unlikely that would be to find, the way things are. But we have space and it's not being used. So, don't you really suppose we should—?"

"You're thinking of putting her in Laura's room?" the old man interrupted, frowning sharply at his wife.

"Yes! It seems like the only decent thing to do. We can't just turn her away! Please say it's all right."

Will Jackson put his frowning stare on Molly for a moment before he told his wife gently, "Why, it's up to you, Sarah. If this is what you want, I guess I got no objection."

She gave him a dazzling smile. "Thank you!" Turning back to Molly, she patted the girl's hand as she said, "You just follow me. I'll show you what we have. I only hope it will please you."

"I'll bring your bag," Boyce Tuthill said.

The Jacksons' little house sat at the rear of the same lot that held their store, but faced on another street. Sarah Jackson led her visitor across a weed-grown yard and, apologizing for taking her in the back way, through a spotless kitchen and along a dark hall. There she opened a door to reveal a room that was pleasantly cool despite the muggy heat outside. She said again, "I hope it will do."

Molly stared. It was a delightful room with crisp curtains and a bright shag rug and a brighter crazy quilt on the bed. There was a dressing table and some comfortable-looking chairs. The effect was entirely homey and inviting.

"Oh, I love it!" Molly exclaimed. "If I were you, I

don't really know if I'd be able to let some complete stranger come into my home and take over a room as nice as this."

"It was our granddaughter's," the woman told her. "She died last winter, of the fever. We've kept it just the way she left it. She would be a little younger than you, but you do very much remind me—" She broke off. Molly, looking at her in alarm, saw that she was biting her lip and blinking hard behind the rimless spectacles. Before Molly could stammer any kind of reply, Sarah Jackson, smiling brightly, abruptly changed the subject. "Have you eaten?"

"Not since breakfast, but—"

"Why, then, you must be starving! As soon as you've settled, come into the kitchen and I'll have something for you."

"Oh, no!" Molly protested. "You mustn't do that!" But the old woman gave her arm a pat and was gone; Boyce Tuthill, arriving just then with Molly's bag, drew aside to let her pass.

He came on into the room, set Molly's bag down at the foot of the bed, and looked around admiringly. "Nice!" he said. "You should be comfortable here."

But Molly faced him with a reproving frown. "You knew! You heard about the granddaughter—and you brought me here on purpose, thinking that because of her these people could be persuaded to take me in."

He appeared puzzled at her accusation. "It was worth a chance. And they did, didn't they?"

"It just wasn't fair to them!"

He seemed surprised by her attitude. "I don't see why. The old lady's happy as a lark, having you here—and why not? Someone young in the house again . . . Whether or not you really do remind these old people of their granddaughter, you're a very nice person, Molly

Bishop! I just don't see how this can do anyone any harm." He added solemnly, "But I'm sorry if you think I was wrong to bring you—I simply didn't know anywhere else! Do you want me to tell them you've changed your mind?"

Slowly she shook her head. "No. You're right, of course—this was the only choice. I'm sorry for what I said: You were trying to help me, and I thank you. I'll do my best not to give this nice couple any reason to regret it. . . ."

When Boyce Tuthill took his leave, satisfied at seeing her comfortable and settled in good hands, she had an idea that she would be seeing him again.

After the poor fare at the stage-line stations, the meal she sat down to in the Jacksons' tidy kitchen seemed as good as a feast. She protested again, but she ate everything her hostess placed before her—good Southern fare, greens and a pork chop, black-eyed peas, and the best cornbread she had tasted in years. Sarah Jackson seemed delighted to see her eat. The old lady kept up a conversation, explaining the accidents of a long life that had brought her and her husband, at last, to keeping a little store in this sleepy village at the deep southern end of Texas. She didn't dwell on the granddaughter whose death, following soon after the passing of their son and his wife, had left them suddenly in old age without any family at all. Nor did she say much about the excitement over the prisoner in the county jail that had changed their town suddenly into a place they hardly recognized.

For her own part, Molly had little to tell except to say as she was finishing her meal, "I don't know yet how long I'm going to be here, perhaps no more than a day or two. But one thing we haven't mentioned yet is how much you're charging me for the room. If you insist on feeding me like this—"

The old woman batted that aside with a wave of a hand. "Now, we won't even mention the food, you hear? As for the rent, that's to discuss with Will. La! I don't know about such things! Just don't fret about it. It's going to be nice having someone to talk to!"

She refused to let her guest lend a hand with the dishes, so presently Molly returned to her room to clean up and change into fresh clothing.

With the good meal and the pleasant talk behind her, she could feel herself beginning to grow tense again. Things could no longer be put off. The moment was upon her when she must face, at last, the purpose that had been all the reason for her coming to Laredo.

Chapter 5

Boyce Tuthill had begun to realize he was talking to a very uneasy and frightened man. When he introduced himself to Harry Swain, the acting sheriff had treated him with considerable suspicion, even after he explained what he was here for and showed his identification. But the fact that Tuthill was a newspaperman from as far away as Kansas City, with connections in St. Louis, soon had its effect in thawing the lawman's manner. Now he sat in the sheriff's office in the two-story county courthouse, notebook on knee and pencil in hand, conducting an interview with the man who had arrested Bart Campion and who had the job of placing him on the gallows at noon tomorrow.

The sound of hammers in the courthouse square came on the stillness of early afternoon. From one window, Harry Swain could look down on the final stages of scaffolding; from another, the small stone jail behind the courthouse was visible. Swain seemed unable to sit still. He kept getting up from his swivel chair for a look first from one window and then the other. He was a gangling, lantern-jawed fellow, a year or two under forty, with a shock of black hair and a mean dark stare. Tuthill suspected he covered weakness with bluster and a show of self-confidence. He was probably a competent paper-server and collector of delinquent taxes, but just now he could be in something that was over his head.

Tuthill found the man's nervousness irritating, but he covered his annoyance and asked his questions with professional deference. "It's been said," he pointed out, "that Bart Campion rode here to Laredo alone, without his gang, for just one purpose—to kill Sheriff Donnelly. Do you know if it was from some personal reason? Or does he simply hate lawmen in general?"

The acting sheriff scowled at his boots at the ends of long legs thrust out in front of him as he sat with his fingers laced across an unbuttoned waistcoat. "That's a tough question. The judge asked him the same thing in court and couldn't get any sort of an answer. All I can tell you is, he's been a surly sonofabitch from the day I took him in. No, I just don't know how he reasons."

"Did Sheriff Donnelly know? You served under him a long time, I understand. If he knew some particular cause why Campion had it in for him, I'd have thought he might have let drop some hint at some time or other."

"Not to me. Ed Donnelly was a good man and a damned good sheriff, but he never was one to say much. I worked for him for six years, and yet I can't honestly say I knew him any better for it. Oh, he was pleased with the way I did my work. But anything personal he kept strictly to himself."

It was not a very satisfactory answer, but Tuthill would have to make do with it. He jotted a note in his book before going on to his next question. "The day Bart Campion was arrested—will you tell me exactly what happened? I understand you, personally, made the capture. I know the readers in Kansas City and St. Louis are

47

going to want to hear, in your own words, exactly how you were able to take a desperate outlaw like that into custody."

As he had guessed, this was a question Harry Swain took considerably more pleasure in answering. Tuthill was sure he had correctly judged him as an ambitious man who saw this interview as an opportunity for glory. "Of course," he said promptly and straightened in his chair, "I'll be glad to tell you what I can.

"Campion showed up here in Laredo on a Saturday afternoon. It's a time when the place fills up with people from out in the county, and of course there's always soldiers from the fort on weekend passes. Campion must have felt he was safe. Even after all this time there aren't many good pictures of him in circulation, so few people would have had any clear idea what he looked like.

"If there was no particular business, Ed Donnelly generally went home early and left things to me or one of the other deputies; but I don't think Campion knew that. Well, it was Buck Studer's turn in the office, and he began to notice this stranger hanging around—just across the street, and then outside the jail, like he was waiting for someone. Since there wasn't much going on, Buck started keeping an eye on him, because of the peculiar way he was acting. Finally the fellow came right into the courthouse, and Buck stepped out in the hall and asked him just what the hell he wanted. He got a look that he told me later almost curdled his blood. The man wanted to know where Ed Donnelly was; Buck said at home. And then the fellow wanted to know where that was. Buck said it never occurred to him he shouldn't tell, but afterward he got to thinking he might have made a mistake. He was worried enough that he came looking for me to let me know what was going on."

Tuthill, scribbling in his notebook, flipped over to a fresh page. "Did *you* have any idea this was Bart Campion?"

"It crossed my mind," Swain admitted. "The description sounded a little like the one good picture of him I'd made a point of studying a few years ago when we were actually holding one of his outlaws in the jail—that was some punk thief who called himself the Salado Kid. But I really couldn't imagine Campion behaving like this. Still, I went hurrying over to the sheriff's house. I was a half block away when I heard the shots—Campion had been waiting in plain sight, and he gunned the sheriff the minute Ed stepped out the door, right there with his wife beside him.

"By the time I arrived, Ed was done for and Campion was starting to mount his horse. We both shot at the same time; he missed, but I didn't. My bullet took him in the shoulder and he dropped his gun, and I just walked up and collared him." Swain added, "There was a dozen other counties wanted extradition so they could try Campion on a variety of charges, mostly bank and stage robberies. But we had the only murder count, and that took precedence. He stood trial, and he was convicted; and tomorrow we hang him."

Hardly had he finished, before Swain was on his feet again for a nervous prowl to the window and another stare outside. Studying the high set of the man's shoulders, Boyce Tuthill thought again that this man wasn't as confident as he tried to sound. He had made a great coup with the capture of Bart Campion, and he had turned the trial and the scheduled hanging into a huge publicity stunt. But perhaps he was beginning to feel he was getting into deeper water than he had intended. Campion's gang might be determined to take revenge on Swain, whether Campion was hanged or escaped.

Tuthill tapped the eraser end of his pencil on the notebook as he commented mildly, "I've been hearing some rumors since I came down here about Campion's outlaws being in the neighborhood."

Harry Swain had swung about. His jaw was thrust forward, his eyes sparked with anger. "The hell with the rumors!" he snapped. "The hell with all the outlaws in Texas! This execution will take place on schedule. You can put it in your paper that Harry Swain said so!"

Oh, yes! Boyce Tuthill thought to himself. *I'll see that it's in there, all right! Whatever happens, or doesn't happen, between then and noon tomorrow.*

Swain's glance had switched suddenly to the doorway, and he said in an altered tone, "Yes? Something you wanted, young lady?"

And Boyce Tuthill looked up in utter surprise as he heard Molly Bishop's voice answer uncertainly, "I hope so. Are you the one in charge?"

"At your service!" The lawman had had a better look at the pretty girl in the doorway. He tugged at the lapels of his waistcoat, where a tin star gleamed faintly. "I'm Harry Swain—acting sheriff of Webb County. How can I help you?"

"Well—" Molly had caught sight of Boyce Tuthill, and as she hesitated he saw her look of dismay. Clearly it had never occurred to her to find him there, and for a moment he thought she would turn and flee, her resolve broken. But then she must have decided she had no choice but to go through with this; she set her shoulders and, resolutely facing Harry Swain, she said in a clear voice, "I

50

understand you're the one holding Mister Campion prisoner. May I see him?"

Tuthill wondered if his expression was as ludicrous as the deputy's. Swain actually blinked, but then his mouth turned stubborn. His first warmth of manner had vanished as he said crisply, "I'm sorry. That's out of the question."

She cried, "Oh, but—please! I *must!*"

Swain shook his head. "Now look, little girl!" he said roughly. "I suppose your friends put you up to this. The town is full of people who'd like a look at that man, but I haven't time to fool with them. Far as the law's concerned, Bart Campion is nothing but a thief and a common murderer. You don't want anything to do with a man like that! So why don't you run along home to your folks?"

Molly Bishop stood her ground, though her voice had an edge of anxiety. "You don't understand! I've come a long way by stagecoach. And it isn't just curiosity. There are reasons why I just have to see him!"

"If you wait till tomorrow, you can see him hang!"

She seemed to wince under the harsh edge of his words. She bit at her lip. "What I'm trying to say is—I need a chance to *talk* to him. Alone . . ."

"Alone?" The man's eyes narrowed. "You wouldn't be trying to put something over on me? Are you sure somebody hasn't *sent* you here—maybe to deliver a message?"

"But—I don't know what you mean!"

"No?" he retorted. "Maybe you aren't supposed to slip Bart Campion the word to be ready when his gang make their try to spring him out of my jail?"

She looked as though she had been struck in the face. Baffled though he was by what he was hearing, Boyce Tuthill stirred himself now to come to her defense. He got

51

to his feet as he protested, "Swain, that's ridiculous! I know this girl. I rode the stage with her all the way from Dallas. I have no idea why she wants to see your prisoner, but I'm positive she could have nothing to do with any gang."

Harry Swain peered sharply from one to the other. He was not too quick-witted, and there seemed too much here for him to absorb. But suspicion was still beating high in him. His jaw set stubbornly and he said in flat tones, "You'll have to convince me, young lady. You go ahead and tell me what you want with Campion; then I'll say whether you get to see him or not."

She hesitated. She protested, "But it's—a personal matter."

"Can't help that. You tell me, or you can forget it!"

Molly Bishop looked into the narrow, suspicious face. At the same time she was all too acutely aware of Boyce Tuthill waiting to hear her answer. He wore a look of real concern, but all the same he had a reporter's notebook and pencil ready to take down whatever she might say. And then, hearing movement at her back, Molly looked quickly around and discovered that voices arguing in the sheriff's office had attracted some of the courthouse hangers-on to gather in the hallway to learn what was happening.

All at once she knew her mission was a hopeless one, doomed from the start. There was no way she could explain it to these men—to this dull-eyed sheriff and the newspaperman looking for a story for his paper and the grinning eavesdroppers in the hall. She felt suddenly stifled and overwhelmed by the folly of her undertaking. All she wanted was to get away from there—abruptly she turned to the door, and something in the look of her caused the men to move apart and let her through. Feeling

their stares, shamed and fighting back tears of humilia-
tion, she hurried through the corridor and out into the
heat of midafternoon.

The idlers who thronged the streets of Laredo eyed
her as she went by, almost running in her haste to get
away, but they let her pass without interference. When she
heard her name called she didn't turn back or lessen her
pace. It was almost half a block away that Boyce Tuthill
finally overtook her. "Molly!" he cried. "Please wait!"
And he caught her by an arm, forcing her to halt.

She stubbornly averted her eyes, reluctant for him to
see the glint of tears. She tucked in her chin and shook her
head as she tried to pull free. "Let me alone!"

"I can't!" he insisted and tightened his grip. "You're
upset. And I want to help you."

"Nobody can help me! I just made a complete fool of
myself. Owen Pryor tried to tell me it was a mistake,
coming to Laredo, and he was right. I should have
listened!"

He was silent a moment. "Pryor told you that, did
he?" He added, "Well, I'm not ready to agree it was a
mistake, because I have no idea why you came. It
certainly would never have occurred to me it was anything
to do with that outlaw in the jail. Molly, I just don't
understand!"

"I wouldn't expect you to," she admitted in a small
voice. She had overcome her first frantic emotion of
flight; she made no more effort to break from him as he
dropped his hand from her shoulder and stood looking at
her.

"The fact remains," Tuthill went on crisply, "if it
means so much for you to see Bart Campion—for
whatever reason—then you'll have to find some way to
get around Harry Swain. He's running this show, and he's

doing it to suit himself. As it happens, he's very much interested right now in the publicity he hopes to get from the story I'm planning to write about him. I think that puts me in a position to have some influence with the man. I'll be willing to see what I can do. But don't you think, first, you really should confide in me?"

A quick suspicion rose in her. *Oh, indeed!* Molly thought bitterly. *I'm sure you'd like to know all about me!* She shuddered at the thought of the story he would likely end up writing—about the mysterious woman who had appeared at Campion's cell on the eve of his hanging to declare herself his illegitimate daughter! Indignation at being used in such a way stiffened her rebellion. Her head lifted and in a voice she managed to keep icily under control she said, "Sorry. I can't do that. Thank you all the same."

She heard him stammer her name, but she was already turning away. She left him without another glance.

Chapter 6

After two hours at the cantina, Owen Pryor convinced himself he was wasting time and getting nowhere. He had spent the time playing solitaire at the corner table with a glass of warm beer going flat at his elbow. He had gone out and walked about the neighborhood to see how much of it he remembered, and he had moved his horse as the shade moved. He had queried the cantina's proprietor without much success.

The man was a new owner. Yes, he knew of rumors that the Campion gang had used this place as a rendezvous on occasion when they were in the area. No, he didn't think he had ever laid eyes on them. When Pryor described Duke Ridge and Merl Loomis, he said yes, he thought they might have been at his bar a couple of nights ago. No, he didn't remember seeing anyone else with them. No, the description of Jim Dance struck no bell at all.

Reluctantly Pryor gave it up; perhaps he would try again later, come evening. He remounted his horse and rode down to the slip and took the ferry to the Texas side. Midafternoon heat lay like a miasma over the shallow surface of the river.

Having asked the ferryman for directions to a certain house on the east side of Laredo, near Zacate Creek,

Pryor headed that way. He was less than a block from the courthouse square when he ran into trouble.

A bunch of men were standing around idly in front of a saloon as he started past; just then a hot blast of wind sweeping through the street flung up a glittering curtain of dust that briefly filled the air blindingly and caused the chestnut to balk and fight the bit. Pryor settled the animal and, when the stinging curtain fell away, he saw Claib Meagher standing in the middle of the street, facing him. Pryor, with other things on his mind, had almost forgotten their encounter at the stage station yesterday, but the big stevedore plainly hadn't. From his aggressive manner he could have been brooding on it. He said loudly, "So, it's you! I thought you were going to look me up when you got to Laredo."

Pryor returned his stare coldly, well aware that the man was looking for an argument. The men who were bunched at the edge of the dirt street were aware of it, too, and they were watching eagerly. But Owen Pryor had no patience for a second run-in with Meagher. He answered briefly. "I said it depended on whether you behaved yourself. Did you?"

The broad face darkened. "You sonofabitch! You figure to teach me manners?"

"It's clear somebody should. But I've got other things to do." Pryor kicked his horse to ride briskly around the other man.

Claib Meagher swore, and as Pryor went by he hooked heavy fingers into the headstall of the chestnut. Impetus carried the animal about in a half circle, hoofs gouging up dust. The horse jerked its head in an effort to break free, but Meagher had a grip of iron. Pryor touched the chestnut on the neck to steady it. In a flat tone he said, "I won't tell you more than once—let go of him!"

56

The big man said, "Get out of that saddle. I'll break you in two!"

More and more of a crowd was being drawn from the saloon and other buildings as they caught wind of something starting. Suddenly it was as though every one of the idlers who had been pouring into Laredo on overcrowded stagecoaches during the past week had collected at this one spot hoping for excitement. Deliberately, Pryor pulled his belt gun—but as he did, a hand reached up from somewhere and without warning clamped upon his arm. When he tried to pull away it held firm. The nervous horse lunged sideward and all at once he felt the saddle go out from under him. He grabbed for the horn, missed, and fell heavily, the gun spilling from his fingers. A voice at his ear said loudly, "Come on and get him, Claib!"

Rolling hastily to hands and knees Pryor looked and saw where his gun had fallen into the dirt, but when he reached for it someone booted it from under his fingers and sent it spinning away. After that he had to scramble to his feet, because Claib Meagher had released the chestnut and was striding toward him. The crowd, seeing a fight, was suddenly yelling eagerly.

Conscious of the yelling voices so earsplittingly close behind him, all shouting encouragement to Meagher, Pryor quickly circled out into the street. He didn't trust a half-drunken mob at his back. The man came on in pursuit, his teeth showing and his big fists clubbed and ready.

Pryor caught a bootheel in a rut and that held up his retreat long enough for the big man to reach him with one of those fists. He managed to pull back so that the blow, aimed for his face, barely grazed it and instead bounced off the point of a shoulder with force enough to turn the whole arm numb. He hit back and struck Meagher in the chest. It was like taking a poke at a wall, but it did hold the man up for a moment. He looked surprised; a gust of breath, carrying the smell of the whiskey he'd been drinking, broke from his open mouth.

The big man caught himself and came on, and this time connected with a glancing blow on the ear that made Pryor's whole head ring. Pryor knew he had to put a quick end to this before those mauling fists really hurt him. They could kill a man, while there seemed no way even of hurting a brute like Meagher. When he caught the gleam of gunmetal in the dust and saw it was his own revolver, he never hesitated. He turned and took a couple of long strides and bent for it.

Just then the frightened chestnut that was moving about and kicking up dust backed between the fighters as someone tried to grab its reins. Claib Meagher let out a roar of fury and struck the animal on the flank, causing it to jump sideward so that it slammed into Pryor as he went for his gun and knocked him sprawling. An iron-shod hoof just missed his ribs. But he had the gun and rolled to his feet. As the dust settled, Meagher found himself staring into the muzzle. It brought him up short.

The excited yelling ended as though cut off by a knife stroke. The street went quiet, without movement— even the horse had come to a halt and stood stomping a hoof, fretting at the bit and dangling reins that held it ground-tied. Meagher had lost some color as he saw the weapon pointed at his head; now he blurted, "Hell! That ain't fair! I got no gun!"

"Well, I've got this one," Owen Pryor said curtly. "And I'll use it! I won't fool with you, Meagher." Pryor was breathing heavily; his ear still rang and his shoulder ached. He smeared a sleeve across the sweat and dirt on his face as he watched Meagher carefully. But sight of the gun had turned the big man cautious, knocking some of the toughness out of him. He stood rooted, glowering narrowly. And Pryor turned and moved a few steps to take his horse by its dangling reins.

A newcomer came shouldering through the crowd. He was hatless, and he had been hurrying. A town marshal's badge pinned to his shirtfront showed in the gap of his unbuttoned waistcoat. He demanded, "What's going on here?"

He looked to be about fifty, a man with a nearsighted stare and a weak mouth. He peered about belligerently, and someone in the crowd said with impatience bred of familiarity, "You stay out of this, Tubman. Nobody pulled your string!"

Marshal Tubman turned red with anger but he didn't try to make a rejoinder. His eyes had lit on the stranger with the gun. At once he dragged a revolver from his own holster and faced Owen Pryor with the other hand outstretched. "I'll take that!"

"No." Deliberately, Pryor put his weapon back into the leather. He was not going to be disarmed by the law or anyone else. "I've done nothing."

The lawman scowled. "That's for me to say. And I say you've been disturbing the peace. You want to make more trouble for yourself by resisting an officer?"

"No. But I won't be arrested for no cause."

One of the onlookers, an older man who didn't seem to be part of the saloon crowd, spoke up then. "He's leveling with you, Marshal. This wasn't his doing. He was just riding by when this big fellow grabbed his bridle and tried to pick a fight. Then somebody pulled him off his saddle, and the big one went after him." And another man added, "That's a fact, Tubman. He was only trying to stop the fight by going to his gun. In his place you'd have done the same."

"Who said that?" the lawman demanded irritably and searched for the speakers. Apparently he recognized someone whose testimony he respected. Wavering, he said with a scowl, "Oh," and lowered his own revolver.

Claib Meagher didn't like the way things were going. He exclaimed loudly, "Don't let 'em lie to you! The sonofabitch was asking for trouble and he got it!" But Marshal Tubman took in the size of him, and then had another look at Pryor, and he didn't seem impressed by the big fellow's argument.

Then Owen Pryor heard a voice he remembered all too well. Something tightened between his shoulders and he turned to look as three more men came striding up.

Gangling, black-haired Harry Swain had changed very little from the time Pryor knew him five years ago. The others with him, judging from the bits of metal pinned on their shirts, were deputy sheriffs of Webb County. Swain was talking loudly, cutting off everybody else as he demanded, "What about it? Do you intend to break this thing up, Marshal, or am I going to have to? We can't allow a disturbance like this practically in front of the courthouse!"

The town marshal was eyeing the county sheriff with ill-concealed dislike. "It ain't a county matter," Tubman snapped back roughly. "Stay out of it. I'll do whatever needs doing." Pryor knew there was frequently a strain in the overlap of authority between town and county-seated law; he wondered if it had been aggravated here in recent days by the undue amount of attention being centered on the sheriff's office. Certainly there was no friendliness in Tubman's manner as he went on to explain curtly, "A

60

couple of men had a difference of opinion, and the rest were yelling them on. It didn't amount to anything."

The acting sheriff looked at Claib Meagher briefly, passed him over, and turned to Owen Pryor; but there his glance halted and his eyes narrowed as he studied the latter's face. Pryor returned the look, keeping his own expression carefully neutral. It wasn't easy. Five years ago this man—a green deputy then—had frequently been given sole charge of a scared youngster named Owen Pryor, who was awaiting extradition and trial and a likely prison term. During those weeks Harry Swain had taken the keenest pleasure in bedeviling his helpless victim. Even now, suddenly meeting the man face to face after all this time, Pryor had to put a firm hold on his emotions.

Harry Swain demanded sharply, "Do I know you?"

"I couldn't say," Pryor answered. "Do you?"

Swain was puzzled and unsure, and it plainly bothered him. Five years had made a difference in Owen Pryor. He had filled out, and his features had fined down. The mustache had grown since his leaving Huntsville Prison and it helped to change his appearance. Familiar as Pryor must look to Swain, it would not be surprising if the acting sheriff failed to recognize him now.

One of the deputies with Swain seemed to be getting nervous. He said into his chief's ear, "Hadn't we better get back, Harry? For all we know this could be a trick, meant to pull us away from the jail!"

Harry Swain made a scornful gesture. "That would be a damnfool thing to try!" But Pryor thought that idea bothered Swain more than he liked to show. Suddenly he seemed in a hurry to have this finished. All officiousness, he turned to the marshal. "We don't need this kind of thing right now, Tubman. Do your job and see we don't have any more of it." With a last look at Pryor—a look that showed the latter still had him baffled and troubled—he warned: "As for you: You'd better try to keep that gun holstered."

"I always try," Pryor replied.

That ended it. Swain and his deputies went tramping off in the direction of the jail as Marshal Tubman began ordering the crowd to break up. No one interfered when Pryor gathered his horse's reins and stepped into the saddle. He gave Meagher a last meaningful look and went on his way.

The house was a simple one, a small, flat-roofed adobe standing not far distant from Zacate Creek that marked the eastern edge of Laredo. It had a neat picket fence around it, a few bright flowers that showed much attention and care. A woman was working on them now. She was rawboned, angular, and utterly graceless in her long skirt and a man's shirt with the cuffs turned back from bony wrists, a bandanna knotted carelessly about her head. The afternoon sun made a silver arc of the spray from the watering can as she moved along the beds, so engrossed in what she was doing that she seemed unaware of Pryor as he reined in beyond the fence and sat watching her a moment.

He said her name: "Mrs. Donnelly . . ."

She straightened. At first there was no recognition, but then the woman's large, expressive eyes seemed to darken. Her head lifted and he saw the displeasure that tightened her bony features. "So!" she said in a dead voice. "It's you!"

"You remember, then. You don't appear pleased to see me."

"Now? Here, in Laredo?" Sheriff Donnelly's widow

shook her head. "I suppose I'm disappointed, since I know why you must have come."

Pryor's own expression hardened a trifle. "You mean, to set Bart Campion loose, I suppose! Well, you happen to be wrong." He lifted the reins. "But I guess I was wrong, too, to have bothered you. Just forget it."

But before he could turn away she halted him with an impatient gesture. "Oh, get down off that horse, Owen Pryor! I haven't had a real look at you."

He did as he was told—he would never have been able to refuse this woman anything. She stepped closer to the gate, the watering can forgotten in her hand while she studied him. Pryor had removed his hat as he stood before her, noting in turn that the passing of five years seemed to have made no change at all in Kate Donnelly. She would be in her late fifties, he supposed, though strong Texas suns must have long since turned her ageless.

She apparently liked what she saw, for she nodded. "You seem to be taking care of yourself. Tie your animal in the shade and let's go inside. No point in our frying out here."

"Thanks." But first he looked around him and asked, indicating the dry growth near the creek bank, "Was that where it happened?"

Face grim, the woman nodded. "He was waiting there when we left the house. There was no warning— nothing. He just stepped out of the brush and fired two shots. According to the doctor, either one would have been enough. Ed was . . . gone before I could even reach him!"

Pryor absorbed that in silence as he looped his reins about a picket of the whitewashed fence and followed Sheriff Ed Donnelly's widow into her house.

It was, just as he would have expected, plain but

comfortably furnished, with an unlighted fireplace, a Mexican rug for a spot of color, a rack in one corner holding Sheriff Donnelly's rifles. The thick adobe walls and narrow windows made the living room dark and cool after the blast of the world outside.

Kate Donnelly got rid of her watering can and joined her visitor on the horsehair sofa. Pryor hated to reopen fresh wounds, but one subject was uppermost in his mind and he thought she would understand his real concern as he asked, "Has no one been able to learn *why* it happened? How Bart Campion could have hated anyone that bad? All I can say is, he must have changed a lot. When I knew him five years ago, I don't think he was capable of doing such a thing: hunting down even his worst enemy and shooting him from ambush, without giving him a chance! And besides that, whenever he mentioned Ed Donnelly it was always with respect—even when he sent me across the river to size up a bank to rob in Ed Donnelly's town!"

"There was a change, all right," the woman agreed, with a deadness coming into her voice as she discussed the killing of her husband. "You may not know that he and Ed were friends once, back before the war—and even afterwards. When Campion first started his one-man crusade against the carpetbaggers, Ed tried to warn him that things could get out of hand sooner or later. He warned him that one day he'd cross the line and earn the label of an ordinary outlaw.

"I think now it may have been the wrong thing to say to him. Very likely Campion always held that warning against my husband—and when the prediction turned out right, he somehow got it into his head that Ed Donnelly was responsible for turning the people of Texas against him. I think Bart Campion got to brooding on that, and finally decided he would get even."

"But—that's crazy!" Owen Pryor exclaimed, aghast.

She answered quietly, "I'm not at all sure that the man I saw sitting in that courtroom like a caged wolf was entirely sane!"

Next moment she got restlessly to her feet, giving his arm a pat and changing the mood as she said, "We need something cool on a day like this. I'm afraid I haven't anything stronger to offer you than some buttermilk from the well house."

"That sounds fine," Pryor said, but his thoughts were a dozen miles away as he waited for her to fetch it.

She brought a tray to put on the table in front of them—a pitcher foaming with cool milk, tumblers, fresh sliced bread with butter. "And some of my plum preserves," she said. "You used to like them, as I remember."

Helping himself, he told her, "I don't think I've tasted anything so good in these past five years."

"Five years . . ." Kate Donnelly repeated. "Has it really been that long?"

"That long. And I'm sure I never told you just what it meant, the way you treated me during the weeks I sat in that jail behind the courthouse. Your husband, too; but you in particular. I'll never forget the meals you fixed, or the hours you spent just listening to me talk, trying to help me straighten out my problems with myself. Of course, I'm sure you'd have done the same for any other scared kid in trouble."

She smiled a little. "I suppose. Still, there was something special about you. Ed and I both felt it. You told me about your pa who used to beat you until you were afraid of what you might do to *him* if you stayed. And then Bart Campion taking you in and treating you decent, and how grateful you felt."

"I wanted to please him," Pryor admitted, a little

grimly, "by being as tough and mean as any member of the gang. I called myself the Salado Kid, and I learned to shoot. But the first job I rode on—I got caught!

"At least," he went on, "I had plenty of time at Huntsville to think things over—all you'd said to me, and what I wanted to do with the rest of my life. When I got out, there was no question of going back to Bart Campion and the gang even if they'd made any effort to keep in touch with me, which they hadn't. I got clean out of Texas and went over to New Mexico Territory where nobody knew me. . . ."

As he ate, he told her something of his cowspread: "It was land nobody else wanted, but it's a beginning." He said he had never been back to Texas until less than a week or so ago, when he rode over to Concho County on the track of a rancher he'd heard was selling out and might let him have some breed stock on terms he could handle. "It was there I learned about Campion being on trial for murdering Ed Donnelly. The minute I heard, I lit out for Laredo as fast as I could get a horse to cover ground."

"And that's what I'm afraid I don't understand," the woman said. "Why *are* you here? Somehow I can't believe it's to watch the hanging!"

"Nor to set him loose, either," Pryor assured her for a second time. "If Campion's gone far enough downhill to murder someone like Ed Donnelly, then he's got to pay for it. No—I came because I reasoned, like a lot of other people, that Campion's gang would be showing up sooner or later."

"And if they did?" she insisted in puzzlement. "What could that possibly matter to you now?"

Pryor set down his empty plate, hesitating over an answer. He said then, "This is something I probably wouldn't talk about to anyone else, but maybe you'll understand. . . . I had a good friend in that outfit, a fellow about like me, maybe a year older. He'd been a cow-puncher, but he had kind of a wild streak. He had trailed up the Chisholm to Abilene one year, but there was a difference of opinion with his boss and he quit without drawing his pay. He was mad, and he was broke. Somewhere later along the line, he fell in with Bart Campion. He was a full-fledged member of the crew when I joined up.

"He treated me well, showed me the ropes, taught me about guns. He even saved my life once—shot the head off a rattler that had got into my blankets. His name was Jim Dance. Do you know of him?"

Kate Donnelly shook her head. "I don't think so. Ed might have."

"I've been wanting all this time to get in touch with him again. I don't know if he's still with the gang—or for that matter, if he's still alive. But this could be my chance. If he's anywhere in the vicinity of Laredo right now I mean to try and find him. I owe him my life."

She was studying Pryor with a sober expression. She sounded dubious as she asked, "Why do you want to see him? Supposing you manage . . . what can possibly come of it?"

"I have a proposition I'd like to make him—that is, if he's interested in listening to it."

"Has it occurred to you," the woman said slowly, "if your friend is still with Campion—after five years—he may not be the person you think you remember?"

Pryor admitted it. "I'm aware of that. I still want to find him. I told you before, I owe him my life. And more than that: Jim Dance was my friend!"

"I see. . . ." Kate Donnelly was silent a moment. Abruptly, she got to her feet and began collecting their dishes onto the tray. " Well, I hope you find him then," she said crisply. "I also hope you'll remember to be careful— and that he's worth the trouble!"

Chapter 7

Pryor had already spotted a public livery stable that looked as though it should serve his needs. He was still preoccupied with the conversation with Ed Donnelly's widow when, leaving the Donnelly house, he rode directly there and dismounted to lead the chestnut through the wide doorway. Belatedly he became aware of a pair of men approaching across the rutted street. He took a second look and halted, instantly on the alert because he recognized them both for deputies he had seen with Harry Swain an hour earlier after his fight with Meagher.

The men were making directly toward him, and he let the horse's reins drop as he stood and watched them come, his face carefully expressionless. He didn't wait for them to declare themselves, but threw a blunt and impatient challenge: "Would you be looking for me?"

That brought them to a wary halt, a few feet distant. They exchanged a look and the one who appeared to be the spokesman answered with a question: "You're the Salado Kid, ain't you?"

"Oh," Pryor grunted. "So Harry Swain finally remembered. . . ."

"All I know is," the man said gruffly, "he give us orders to hunt you up and fetch you in." They looked as though they might have been warned that this wouldn't necessarily be an easy thing to do. Wearing deputy sheriff's badges didn't make them more than ordinary men, who were of only ordinary daring. They kept shooting glances back and forth, as though they needed to reassure themselves they had a two-to-one advantage. Each wore a holstered gun but so far neither seemed anxious to be first to touch a weapon.

Seeing their uneasiness, Pryor asked impatiently, "Just where do I stand? Am I under arrest?"

The second deputy cleared his throat. "Harry never said nothing about that. He only said to bring you."

If they did that, the next step was obvious: Vagrancy, or suspicious behavior—almost any charge would serve to justify throwing Pryor into jail and leaving him there until the deadline at noon tomorrow had passed and Campion was safely hanged. To Harry Swain it would probably seem a natural precaution to take with a man he knew to have been a member of Bart Campion's gang—natural to assume that he could be here in Laredo for only one purpose.

But Owen Pryor had no intention of letting himself be taken in to increase Harry Swain's peace of mind. He shook his head and told these two, "Nothing doing. I have no business with Harry. I've broken no laws in Webb County. He's got no call to give me orders."

"But *our* orders—" the first man began, scowling with confusion. Pryor cut him off.

"Your orders mean nothing to me! The only way you'll ever arrest me is with a legal bench warrant— and my name on it."

"Look here!" But the protest died as Owen Pryor dropped his hand to the butt of his holstered weapon. Seeing that, the man almost stammered, "Now, listen! We don't want gunplay!"

"If you figure to arrest me," Pryor told him curtly, "you're apt to get some. So, leave me alone—I'm in no mood for this!"

Neither deputy seemed ready to challenge the advantage in that hand resting on a gun butt. The second man gave his companion a muttered suggestion: "What do you think? Maybe we better go back and talk to Harry."

"If you do," Pryor put in, "tell him I said he's mistaken about me. I didn't come here to make trouble. That's straight, let him believe it or not!" He didn't suppose this protest would do any good with Swain, but he felt better for making it.

The first man seemed reluctant to back down, but his companion tugged nervously at his sleeve and said, "Come on, Buck!" And hesitantly, Buck at last gave way. They turned and walked back across the street the way they had come, with scowling looks across their shoulders. Pryor stood and watched them go. They passed around a corner and out of sight.

He turned again to his horse and, as he took the reins, saw he had had an audience.

In the livery entrance, a red-bearded man and a half-grown Mexican youth who was apparently his hostler were watching Pryor with expressions of pure pleasure—they had probably seen the whole encounter, and they didn't care who might know their satisfaction at watching the deputies taken down a peg. Nobody mentioned it, however, by so much as a word, but the bearded liveryman listened with respect as Pryor asked him, "Can I put my animal up here for a night or two? He's been working hard. He could use a good graining and a rubdown."

"You heard the man," the livery owner told his

assistant, and the Mexican lad bobbed his head and took the reins, to lead the chestnut into the dimness of the barn. "That rear stall is empty," the man called after him. "Put him in there."

"I might want him again, later this evening," Pryor said. "I'm not certain. Meanwhile, I was wondering: Would it be worth an extra dollar to let me bed down in your hayloft? I doubt I can find a room anywhere in this town, and I've had enough for now of sleeping in the brush!"

The bearded man was more than agreeable. They settled on a price, and Pryor paid in advance and left.

The long afternoon was dragging out to an end, the slanting light touching the dusty streets and drab buildings with gold, the shadows stretching black and long; there was no easing at all in the breathless heat. As Pryor walked through town he was oppressed by a sense of wasted time. He was at loose ends, completely unsure of his next step.

When he brought the courthouse square into view, he saw an even larger crowd than had been there earlier. Wary to avoid another encounter with Harry Swain or his deputies, he drifted closer and saw that the scaffold, completed now, was in the process of being tested. There was Swain and another man Pryor took to be the executioner—a professional hangman, no doubt, hired and brought in for the job. With a cold feeling of distaste Pryor watched a loaded sandbag hoisted up in place. At a signal a lever was pulled, a catch tripped. The trapdoor plunged open. . . . He turned away as a roar of approval went up from the crowd, and he caught sight of a man who was busily setting up a camera on a tripod, with a box of glass plates ready on the ground beside him. His camera seated squarely on its legs, the photographer ducked under the black cloth that draped it while he sized up his shot. Boyce Tuthill stood by, watching and offering suggestions. The reporter from the Kansas City *Journal of Commerce* looked around as Pryor came toward him.

Pryor said, "Where did you unearth a photographer?"

Tuthill nodded toward a horse and wagon that stood nearby—a traveling studio and darkroom under weather-streaked canvas. "The man's an itinerant," he said. "Came to town hoping to get some pictures tomorrow he could peddle. I've made a deal with him for first pick of anything I can use with my story."

"Well," Owen Pryor observed, "I'd say there's no doubt you'll go far in this business. You don't miss many angles!"

The man with the camera inserted a plate and went under the cloth again as the trapdoor was lifted into place and the sandbag lugged back up the wooden steps for another trial. Pryor turned his back on this operation and changed the subject. "Did Molly Bishop arrive all right? No more trouble, I hope."

Tuthill's quick glance held more than a hint of jealousy, but he answered, "You mean from our friend Meagher, I suppose. No—no trouble." He added, "I did hear that he got into a fight on the street a little while ago with someone that answered your description. Now, could that have been you?"

"It could," Pryor answered shortly. "And, Molly? Where is she now?"

The other man seemed reluctant for him to know. "Staying with some people named Jackson—they have a grocery over on San Bernardo. Damnedest thing," he

73

continued in a puzzled tone. "She came to the sheriff's office while I happened to be there. And would you believe, she wanted to see Campion!"

Pryor showed no reaction. He simply asked, "Did she get to?"

"No. The acting sheriff, fellow named Swain, sent her packing—wouldn't even listen. I tried to talk with her afterwards but she was terribly upset. I couldn't get a thing out of her!" He looked at Pryor narrowly. "You know, I saw the two of you talking together quite a while last evening at the stage station. Maybe you know something, like what business she could possibly have with Bart Campion?"

Pryor looked at the other man levelly. "Afraid not," he lied without hesitating. If Molly Bishop had wanted Boyce Tuthill to know her affairs, she would have told him herself.

He found the grocery already closed for the night, but on asking questions was sent around the corner to the next street. The Jackson residence was a small frame house, painted white, with a deep veranda covered with vines that rattled in the summer heat. Dusk was not far away as he stepped up on the porch and knocked; the tiny woman who opened the door eyed him uncertainly.

He asked, removing his hat, "Is Miss Molly Bishop here? Please, I'd like a word with her if she is. You can tell her it's Owen Pryor."

"Well . . ." She looked askance at his dusty boots and trail-stained clothing and holstered gun before suggesting, with a hint of reluctance, "Would you care to step inside?"

"No, I'll wait out here. I'm not dressed for anybody's parlor." He didn't add that if for any reason Molly decided she would rather not see him, it would be less embarrassing for him to take his departure from the porch.

But he had waited only moments when light footsteps came hurrying and then the girl herself was there, stepping out to greet him with every evidence of pleasure. "I hardly expected to see you again!" she exclaimed as she took his hand.

"I couldn't have left without knowing for sure how things had gone for you," he said.

"But however did you find where I was?"

"I ran into Boyce Tuthill; he told me."

"Oh. I see."

Hesitantly, Pryor added, "He told me something else, too. About what happened at the courthouse."

Abruptly her smile faded, her manner changed. "No—I don't suppose he *could* keep that to himself!"

"Only because he was concerned about you," Pryor insisted. "And so am I. Knowing what you came here for, I was afraid you wouldn't have an easy time of it."

"Yes, you told me it was a mistake to come—and you were right, of course. This horrible town!" she cried in sudden bitterness. "I *hate* the place. . . . Mr. and Mrs. Jackson have been very kind, but, aside from them—"

Pryor laid a sympathetic hand on her shoulder. "I know how tired and discouraged you must be, Molly," he said earnestly. "And with this mob that's taken over, you couldn't be blamed for not liking what you've seen of the place. For that matter, I've no reason to have any great love for it myself! But you know, you haven't really seen the true Laredo. It has another side that I'd like to show you," he added on an impulse. "If you have a moment, it's only a few blocks from here. Will you come?"

She looked at him closely, as though trying to fathom what he had in mind. But she felt she could trust him, and she nodded. "Of course." She took his arm, and let him lead her down from the porch to the street.

Day was almost gone; lamplight already bloomed in windows and open doorways and the first grainy dusk lay upon the streets as they turned in the direction of the river. Molly said suddenly, "Do I hear music?" Pryor only smiled. The clarion sound of a cornet, right at the top of its register, grew louder as they approached. Now they could hear the voices of fiddles and a guitar, not all quite in tune. And, very near the drop-off of the bluff above the Rio Grande, a plaza the size of a city block opened before them.

There were trees and a crisscross of graveled walks, and in the center of the open space stood a tiny bandstand. The music came from there—a handful of instruments pouring a lively cantina melody into the quiet evening. Late sunlight still lingered in the trees and gilded the facade of an old adobe church that rose on the plaza's eastern side and was surrounded by scaffolding that indicated the building was either in the process of repair or about to be torn down and replaced. Under the trees the shadows were lengthening amid a glow of lanterns and lamplit windows about the square.

And there were the people, young Mexican men and girls for the most part, decked out in their best apparel. Bright dresses wove color into the evening as they made their leisurely and segregated promenade about the central bandstand—moving in opposite circles, the girls chattering among themselves and pretending not to notice the young men, but thoroughly aware of the looks they received. Seated comfortably on benches about the edge of the plaza, a phalanx of older women kept careful watch over their daughters.

Molly Bishop exclaimed, "However did you know about this?"

"I happened onto it once, some years ago," Pryor explained briefly. "You may not realize it, but right now you're looking a couple of centuries into the past of Old Mexico. I understand Augustin Plaza was the heart of the first settlement here on the Rio Grande—the Mexicans say Rio Bravo. And for more than a hundred years the young people have done their courting here, just like this. As you can see, twice in every tour around the plaza a person can get a glimpse of the one he's taken a fancy to. Signals can get passed that way. Eventually a lot of marriages have come out of this old ritual. I sort of thought you'd find it interesting."

"It's charming!" she exclaimed. "And I do thank you—I'm glad I didn't miss it."

Molly seemed to have been lifted out of her depressed mood of a few minutes ago; when she turned her smile on him, Pryor caught his breath as he was struck by the dazzling way it transformed her. Turned quickly self-conscious he said gruffly, "Here's a bench. Maybe we could sit awhile."

The musicians finished their number, and the guitar player took up the task alone, accompanying himself with a cascade of liquid notes as, in a slight but true tenor voice, he sang the words of some ancient Spanish love song. The ballad and the tinkling notes of the guitar added brightness to the settling dusk.

A voice said, "Well! Hello!"

Pryor got to his feet as he turned, taken by surprise. The newcomer was Boyce Tuthill. He told them, "I didn't expect to find the two of you here. I heard the music and dropped down to see what was going on."

Pryor asked, "How did the pictures turn out?"

"They haven't been developed yet; I'll see them later. I want to get an idea what kind of work that photographer does before I actually make a deal with him."

Molly had caught one word out of the exchange. "Pictures?" she said, looking from one to the other curiously. Owen Pryor scowled. He didn't think she needed to hear that a photographer would be on hand tomorrow to catch the image of Bart Campion dropping from the gallows. Luckily, at that moment the band struck up another tune and the subject was changed as Tuthill's attention was caught by the colorful scene before them. He seated himself next to the girl and Molly began to explain what she had just learned from Pryor. Photography was forgotten.

The sky above the treetops had turned flat and pale as steel as the last color faded from it and a star or two appeared. The off-key sounds of the little band lifted through the dusk. The languid circling of the brightly dressed young people in the plaza continued.

Something struck the bench lightly and pattered away unnoticed. Moments later a second stone, better aimed than the first, plucked at Pryor's sleeve and he jerked his head about. Instantly he caught sight of the man who stood in a tree's shadow, face dimly visible against the growing dusk—a man in the hat and boots and jeans of an ordinary cowpuncher, with a holstered gun strapped against his leg. Pryor knew at once who it was. He stared, motionless with surprise. The man in the shadows raised a cupped hand to his mouth and gave a toss of the head, pantomiming the motion of taking a drink. Next moment he had turned and was gone, drifting away into the darkness.

Tuthill intruded on Pryor's thoughts. The reporter had questions: How much did he know about the early history of Laredo? When was the town built? Pryor answered with no more than half his mind on it, saying it was around 1750 when the first settlement was begun here on the north bank of the river, only afterward spilling over into Nuevo Laredo on what was now the Mexican side of the Rio Grande. Having said that much, he broke off abruptly to tell the other man, "That's about all the history I know. Anyway, I can't stay any longer right now—there's something I have to do. Will you see to it that Molly gets back safely?"

"More than happy to," Tuthill assured him. Pryor caught Molly's puzzled look. The girl started to say something but he couldn't wait for it and didn't notice the quick shadow of hurt and disappointment that clouded her eyes. He was already turning away, without another word, and hurrying in pursuit of the vanished Jim Dance.

Chapter 8

The block held two saloons. Pryor tried the first without finding the man he sought among the early crowd at the bar or sitting at the tables. But three doors farther along he stepped through the wide-open entrance of a second establishment, whose slatted batwings were hooked back to allow any stirring of air to move, and there he struck pay dirt.

Jim Dance sat alone at the far end of the long room, where he could have his back to the adobe wall and an immediate view of anyone who entered. A bottle and a couple of glasses were on the table, and he had a deck of cards and was shuffling them with easy skill. When he caught sight of Pryor he nodded and gestured, and as the latter started toward him through the noisy press of men and the blue drifts of tobacco smoke that hung stale and heavy, Dance picked up the bottle and poured drinks for them both.

There was no exchange of greetings; it might have been yesterday when they last met. Dance gave the old grin that Pryor remembered and said on a genial note, "I heard you was looking for me."

"You must have run into Longley."

Dance admitted it. "I might not have known you

otherwise. That mustache makes a hell of a lot of difference."

Pryor let himself into the chair opposite as the other man took up his glass and saluted him with it before quickly draining it off. He was broad of face, youthful of appearance; he had the kind of sandy hair that usually begins to retreat early from the temples, but it wasn't noticeably any thinner now than it had ever been. His cheeks held a reddish glint of wiry whiskers—he had always been careless about shaving, as were most men of that time and place. With a sweat-stained range hat pushed back on his head, wearing a colored shirt, unbuttoned vest, and denim pants, and with scuffed boots crossed comfortably under the table, Jim Dance could have been a puncher in off one of the Webb County ranches—until you looked closer at the wooden-handled gun in his oiled holster and the dangling thongs for tying it securely into place against his leg.

Pryor took his own drink more slowly, rather from politeness than because he actually wanted it. He shook his head and placed his palm over the empty glass when he saw Dance had the bottle poised, ready to fill it again. At that, his friend let his grin widen. "Did the pokey turn you into a one-drink man?" he suggested. His own glass was already filled to the brim and he tossed it off. He had downed two drinks since Pryor entered and probably more earlier; but he was a man who enjoyed his liquor and could hold a lot of it without showing any effect.

He said, "Bill Longley tells me you gone back to cowboying."

"That's true," Pryor said. "Except that I got my own spread now in New Mexico. Deeded land with water on it, some timber, and government range for grazing my beef.

In a few years it can be built up into a fair little outfit."

"Good for you." But next moment Dance added, his attention shifting from Pryor to someone he had caught sight of in the crowd, "Hey! Here's the man I been laying for! He took a couple hundred off me last night, and I promised him then I'd be getting even. How about it?" he added. "Want to sit in on a little five-handed stud?" He was already reaching for the deck of cards, and Pryor was seized by quick alarm.

"Wait!" He caught his friend's arm as Dance seemed about to call the man over. "I'm not in Laredo to play poker! I rode a lot of miles in a hurry to get here, and now time is short and I need a word with you—alone. Can't we go somewhere and talk things over?"

Something in Pryor's manner seemed to get through to the sandy-haired man. Dance looked at him closely and saw that he was in earnest. Briefly reluctant, the outlaw shrugged then and pushed the cards away. "That sounds fair. Sure—why not? Plenty time for a game . . ." He shoved back his chair. "Let's go, then."

Since he had paid for the bottle, Dance took it along. He had a horse waiting at the tie pole outside—a black, wearing a Mexican charro saddle with a silver horn that looked only slightly smaller than a pie plate; he took the reins and, instead of mounting, led the horse as he conducted Pryor deeper into this oldest, Mexican section of town.

They hadn't far to go. In front of an adobe shack, set a little apart from its neighbors with butter-yellow lamplight spilling from its few tiny windows, Jim Dance dropped the reins to ground-anchor his animal and stepped up to the crude slab door that stood ajar. He nudged it wide with the toe of one boot, and as he stood framed against the light within he was greeted by a cry of surprise and pleasure: "Jaime! But you are back so early!"

Jim Dance said, in an amused tone, "You didn't really suppose I could stay away from you, Conchita?" He turned then to give Pryor a summoning jerk of the head.

"I've brought somebody with me," he said, and the other man, somewhat reluctantly, followed him inside.

The shack was as impoverished as any Pryor had seen. It contained odds and ends of furniture, and there was a mud fireplace that served for cooking and, whenever necessary in this climate, for heating. There were still some coals from a recent cook fire. Even with door and windows open to any slightest hint of breeze along the river flats, the heat in the low-ceilinged main room was almost stifling.

The room's sole occupant was the girl. She was a beauty, barelegged and olive-skinned and obviously very young. She wore a skirt and a loose blouse, and her raven-black hair was free to her shoulders. Jim Dance caught her with an arm about her waist, pulled her to him, and kissed her vigorously; but her warm greeting turned uncertain as she caught sight of the stranger. Releasing her, Dance said, "This here's the Salado Kid. He's an old friend of mine so I want you to be nice to him. I bet he could use a bowl of that chili you dished up for me a little earlier. And then you better run along till I call you. The Kid and I have some talking we need to do."

If she resented Pryor, the girl offered no objection. She seemed used to taking orders from Jim Dance. Without another word she filled a bowl from the iron pot on the fireplace hook, placed it on the crude deal table along with a spoon and a plate of cold tortillas. Ignoring any thanks, she gave Pryor the briefest of glances and padded silently into the adjoining room, closing the door behind her.

Dance motioned Pryor to the food, pulled out another chair for himself, and set his whiskey bottle in front of him.

Pryor had eaten a large meal at noon, but he had missed enough meals lately so that he was ready for another. But he mildly protested, "I hadn't meant to invite myself in for free grub."

Dance waved that aside. "No problem. Conchita don't mind. She's a good sort. Her pa don't amount to much, ain't hardly ever around. Which is all right with me." He pulled a tin cup toward him, splashed whiskey into it, then let it sit as he looked thoughtfully at his friend. "All right. Let's hear what's on your mind, Kid."

As he ate, Owen Pryor commenced to talk.

This moment was the goal that had drawn him here, and all the eloquence he possessed went into his description, in detail, of his achievements and his hopes for the ranch in New Mexico. But as he spoke he knew it wasn't good enough. Jim Dance was listening attentively, his pale eyes studying the other man's face, and yet Pryor had a sense of a wall going up, a shield that his words couldn't really penetrate. Finally, as he paused for breath, Dance said with a trace of impatience, "You already told me most of this earlier. It does sound like you been putting a lot of work into that place, and I sure hope it pays off. But what has it all got to do with me?"

Owen Pryor braced himself. "To tell you the truth, I was hoping you'd want to come in with me on it."

Dance's cool expression showed no change. "Who, me?" he echoed. "Go back to cowboying?"

84

"Not cowboying," Pryor insisted quickly. "Ranching! There's all the difference in the world, if you're sweating for yourself and not just for beans and thirty a month while some other gent gets rich. When it's your own spread you'll work twice as hard as you ever did on a payroll, because it's for something beyond a month's paycheck and Saturday night in town to blow it."

Dance's pale eyes narrowed slightly. "And all this that you've been building—you mean you'd split it with me?"

"Fifty-fifty. Down the middle."

"And why would you want to hand me half?"

"It's no free gift. Don't worry—you'd earn your split. The thing is, two men could make the place go better than one man can working alone. You can believe me, I've given the thing a lot of thought. I've reached the stage where I could sure use a partner—and my first choice is you."

"I don't see why," Dance insisted. "Hell, it's been five years since you and I so much as laid eyes on each other!"

"Well, for one thing, you saved my life."

"I did?" The other man seemed genuinely surprised to hear it. But then he said gruffly, "Oh—I suppose you mean that business with the rattlesnake. You don't owe me anything. It's long forgotten."

"Not by me," Pryor said. "But leaving that aside— you and I are friends, Jim! Nothing's ever changed that, far as I'm concerned, and I hope it never does. Trouble is, since I left prison I haven't known any way to get in touch with you—not until this business at Laredo gave me a reason to think I just might run across you here. Anyway, it seemed worth the gamble and I took it; I was that anxious for a chance to make you my offer."

"An offer to bust my butt chasing cattle again?" A corner of Dance's mouth twitched wryly.

"Wait!" Pryor held up a hand. "Before you say no, let me ask you: What better do you have to look forward to? What can you show for your last five years with Bart Campion, outside of a shotgun blast that nearly killed you? And how about five years from now?

"I wouldn't try to lecture you, Jim, just because I served my time in Huntsville. Even so, I can tell you it's a damn good feeling to be square with the world, not having to hide your campfire, not taking a second look at any man with a piece of metal pinned to his coat front!"

"Maybe," Dance said harshly, "you want me to turn myself in! Spend the next five or ten years in Huntsville . . . Is that what you'd like?"

"Not even for my worst enemy!" Pryor's answer was quick and heartfelt. "But think, Jim! In New Mexico Territory your slate is clean. Nobody there knows you at all, any more than they knew about the Salado Kid. You can take another name if you want to. As my partner, nobody'll ever connect you with the Campion gang.

"All you have to do is say the word. If you like, I can throw a saddle on my horse and we'll leave here now, tonight—get out while the gettin's still good. How about it, Jim? Is it a deal?"

Having made his plea he could only wait for his friend's decision. Owen Pryor hadn't let himself voice his real conviction that this could be the last option for Jim Dance. If he refused, there might never be another chance to turn back from the course he was on or make a last clean break for a new start. Anxiously Pryor watched as the other man sat scowling at the table top. The cup still held his unfinished drink. Dance picked it up, swirled its contents. Then, slowly, he shook his head.

"Afraid not, Kid," he said, and Pryor's heart turned leaden. "You got the best intentions in the world. But it just don't appeal to me, the idea of working myself into the ground eighteen hours a day—for what? I couldn't stand knowing all the fun I was missing, and likely not even a dime in my jeans for a drink of a Saturday evening or energy enough to even look at a poker hand—"

"It wouldn't be as bad as that," Pryor tried to argue, but he knew the cause was lost.

"Bad enough!" Dance retorted. "You may as well forget about counting me in. I can't change now. I got to have the excitement and money enough for good liquor and a high stakes game when I find one!" He tossed off his drink, almost defiantly; then, without meeting Pryor's eye, he added in an altered tone, "Do you need to hear more? Maybe the truth is, it's gone too long. Maybe I just haven't the guts anymore to face that kind of a challenge!"

So Pryor gave it up, his shoulders settling, his body and spirit heavy, defeated. Dance had spoken honestly and with finality. In that moment, his pretenses were down. Yellow lamplight showed revealing signs of disillusionment, the lines about the eyes that made him look older than his years. Pryor took a breath. "I'm sorry." There appeared to be nothing more he could add to that.

Abruptly, Jim Dance showed a complete change of mood. Suddenly he was grinning, in jovial spirits again. "No hard feelings, Kid," he said. "Hell, it ain't the end of the world. Have a drink, and let's have Conchita fetch her guitar and do us a tune. Or we can go set up that game of stud I mentioned."

"No." Pryor pushed his chair back, moving heavily. "I guess not, Jim. I'm not in the mood—and it don't look like you and I have got much left to say. . . ." He broke off as a sound at the open doorway made him turn. One look at the pair of men who had entered and instantly he was on his feet. Jim Dance, for the moment, was forgotten.

Chapter 9

He recognized the pair who halted just within the opening—he wouldn't have needed the word from Bill Longley that they were in the neighborhood. But they looked at him as at a stranger, and Merl Loomis demanded suspiciously, "Who is this, Jim? I don't know him."

"Don't you?" Jim Dance said. "Look again."

The second of the newcomers, whose name was Duke Ridge, let his frown give way to sudden surprise. "Well, by God!" he exclaimed. "It's the Kid. It really is!" He advanced quickly. Loomis still held back. He hadn't failed to notice the hand that rested, as a precaution, on the butt of Pryor's holstered gun.

No one offered to shake hands. Ridge was surveying Pryor closely, as though tallying the changes he saw in him. Duke Ridge himself appeared to have altered little. He was one of the oldest members of the gang and had been generally accepted as second-in-command. He would be over forty now, a man shorter than Pryor but solidly built, with a bullet-shaped head and heavy brows and an aggressive thrust to his jaw. But Owen Pryor had always suspected that to be a cover for a certain indecisiveness that tended to show itself under stress.

Ridge shifted his stare to Jim Dance now and demanded, "What about this, Jim? Where the hell did you find him?"

"He just showed up. First I knew about it, I heard on the grapevine he was here and looking for some of the old gang."

"He found us," Merl Loomis said. Still pointedly eyeing the hand that lay on Pryor's gun butt he added, "And he looks set for trouble!"

"Only being cautious," Pryor corrected him. "How could I know the reception I'd get? A lot of things can happen in five years."

Ridge repeated that in a tone of surprise. "Has it really been five years! How long you been out of Huntsville, Kid?"

"A while."

"Maybe," Loomis suggested bluntly, "you'd like to hold it against us for you letting yourself get picked up and sent there?" That earned him Pryor's full attention for a silent moment. There had been something like bad blood between these two from the day Pryor—a green youngster—first joined the gang. As far as Loomis was concerned, that hostility didn't seem to have altered with time. He was as belligerent as ever.

Duke Ridge rubbed a palm across the stubble on his jaw. "Kind of too bad, the way it worked out for you, Kid. I've wondered about you some, in the years since. You just seemed to drop clean out of sight. Nobody knew if you was still inside, or if you'd finally got out, or what the hell had happened."

"I've been taking care of myself," Owen Pryor assured him briefly. "I expect to keep on."

Merl Loomis might have made some remark at that,

but just then the door to the other room opened. The girl, Conchita, had heard this burst of new voices, and judging from the look of her she didn't much like what she saw. She said something to Dance in her own tongue, whereupon Ridge told the young fellow irritably, "Get rid of her. We don't need an audience."

Dance seemed reluctant, but with a shrug he rose and went to speak to the girl. In the Spanish that was apt to be a second language with anyone who spent much of his life along the border, he assured her they wouldn't be long—just give them a few minutes to settle some business. . . . She didn't fancy being ordered out of her own kitchen. Snatching a shawl from its peg she flung it about her shoulders and went flouncing out, slamming the door behind her. Afterward Pryor turned to the others and, with a start, found Merl Loomis's gun out of its holster and pointed squarely at him.

Dance saw and reacted hotly. He swung about as he cried out, "Loomis! Damn you—"

The narrow-faced outlaw, not taking his baleful stare from Pryor, said, "We're getting nowhere! I want this man to tell us what he's doing in Laredo, and I better like what I hear! I never trusted him and I don't now!"

"Put that away!" Ridge snapped, and after a moment Loomis grudgingly obeyed. Ridge told Pryor, "Try not to blame him too much. The bunch of us is strung tight enough right now to go after each other's throats over nothing. Me, I'm right pleased about running into you, Kid. You ain't said so, but you and us have got to be here for the same reason—we know we can't let them go through with this business tomorrow!"

Pryor returned his look. "You really think you can stop a hanging? Because, one thing certain, you'll never

break Bart Campion out of the Laredo jail. I've got reason
to know. Don't forget, I've seen that building from the
inside!"

Ridge scowled. Before answering he stepped to the
table, picked up the bottle and the cup Jim Dance had
been drinking from, and poured himself a shot of
whiskey. The others watched in silence while he drank,
and Owen Pryor thought suddenly, *He's under a worse
strain than he wants to let on!* Rather like Harry Swain, in
the sheriff's office, Ridge could be a competent second-in-
command; but maybe he wasn't big enough to fill this role
that had been thrust upon him as the brains and leader of
the gang.

Tossing down his empty cup Duke Ridge informed
him, "Busting the jail don't even enter into it, Kid. It's
surprise we're counting on. The way we've set it up—"

"Duke!"

The warning almost exploded from Merl Loomis,
but it had no effect. Ridge, anxious perhaps to convince
himself as well as a skeptical Salado Kid, plunged ahead
as though he hadn't been interrupted: "We've got better
than a dozen men; the rest are in camp tonight, a few miles
from town. Just before noon we plan to start moving in.
Our best riflemen will take positions on roofs overlooking
the courthouse square. There they'll have a crossfire over
the crowd and the door of the jail and the space around
the gallows. Minute the sheriff's men bring Bart outside,
they open up. Once the guards are picked off they'll start
to work on the crowd.

"That should start a real panic, and it'll be the cue for
the rest of us to come barreling in, pick up Bart, and head
for the river before anybody knows what's happening.
The confusion will give the boys on the rooftops time to

reach their horses. Whole thing should be over in a matter of minutes and the lot of us on our way to Mexico. It's as simple as that."

Owen Pryor could only stare at him as he heard this bizarre scheme. Merl Loomis was almost shaking with rage. "For the love of God!" he cried. "Do you have to go and blab every damn thing you know?"

Again Duke Ridge ignored him. His whole attention was on Pryor and now he said, "You *are* coming in on it with us? We can use every extra man—"

Pryor shook his head. "Sorry. Count me out."

His refusal was met by a stunned silence. Loomis was the first to speak. A sneer touched his mouth as he suggested, "Maybe it sounds too rough for you, Kid? You've turned a little yellow?"

Pryor only looked at him, not letting himself be goaded. "No," he said coldly. "But I'm not taking part in any jail break."

"Not for Bart Campion?" exclaimed Ridge.

"Not even for him. He murdered a better man than any of us in cold blood. Most people would say he's only getting what he deserves." Owen Pryor added, "For what *I* did, all I drew was two years in prison. But I came out of there a different man. I served my time, and I've hewed straight to the line ever since. I can't help it if you jumped to a wrong conclusion about what brought me to Laredo."

"Then what the hell did, if it wasn't to do with Bart?" Ridge asked.

"A private matter." He glanced at Jim Dance, and a trace of bitterness found its way into his voice. "It turned out I had some things figured wrong, myself. They didn't work out, and it doesn't give me much call to hang around this town any longer." He added, "If we've got no more business, I'll be saying adios."

He reached for his hat on the table where he'd laid it. As he picked it up he caught a movement from the corner of his eye. Merl Loomis had taken a stride toward him, a hand dropping to his holstered gun. "Not so fast!" he cried, anger heating up his eyes. "Damn you, you aren't leaving this room unless we say so! You don't really think we'd let you go and, like as not, spill everything you've heard to that bunch at the courthouse!"

Pryor looked at him, refusing to show any fear of that undrawn weapon. "You think that's what I have in mind?"

"I suppose you'll deny it? After telling us what kind of a damned law-lover you've turned into!"

But Jim Dance had had enough. He shoved himself between them, letting his elbow strike Merl Loomis and force him back. "You've got this dead wrong!" he said sharply. "Don't listen to him, Duke!" he added, appealing to Ridge who had remained motionless by the table. "After everything the Kid's gone through on account of this outfit, he could hardly be blamed for not having any love for it. But that don't make him a traitor! Besides, he never asked to hear all that stuff—you went ahead and spilled it without bothering to sound him out first. Now anyone who says he can't leave will have to deal with *me!*"

Owen Pryor thanked him with a glance, but with a shake of the head as well. He didn't want his friend risking a fight on his account.

Merl Loomis looked ready for one, but instead he appealed to the third member of the gang. "What about it, Duke?" he demanded harshly. "You claim to be running this outfit. Then speak up! Are you willing to let this man walk out on us knowing what he does? Hell, man—do something!"

But Duke Ridge only scowled, a scowl of complete indecision. And Pryor, seeing the division among them, knew this was the moment to act. Saying firmly, "I can't stand around and wait while you thrash it out. I'm going!" he turned and walked directly to the door, every nerve and muscle tensed to meet a move to stop him.

It never came. He lifted the latch and, his hand on the open door, he turned back to the three pairs of eyes on him and offered a reminder: "Anybody that might try coming after me would make a good target against the light!" He gave that just long enough to sink in. After that he opened the panel wide enough to slip through and pulled it shut behind him.

By lamplight through the window he had a brief glimpse of the girl, Conchita. She stood in shadows with the shawl over her dark hair, eyeing him with a melancholy expression. Next moment she vanished into darkness as someone in the house suddenly blew the kitchen lamp.

That was all the warning Owen Pryor needed.

An open stretch of weeds and barren ground separated this shack from its nearest neighbor. He set off at a dead run along the twisting pathway, but before he could reach that other building he heard the door behind him flung open amid excited shouting. That must have roused some curious person, for in the house ahead of Pryor a shuttered window opened. A wash of light spilled out. He knew he had been caught by it when a pair of gunshots came after him, sounding almost together.

He flinched, half-expecting one or the other bullet to find him. But he was untouched and he plunged ahead, and when he crossed the front of the building he turned aside. There was a slot between it and another of the Mexican quarter's adobe shacks, and having taken several steps he halted and set his back against the mud wall, able to feel through the cloth of his shirt the day's lingering heat held by the dried mud bricks. Making as narrow a shape as possible, he drew his gun and waited, controlling his breathing.

Almost at once he heard the nearing sound of footsteps and his pursuers burst into sight at the forward end of the slot. There were two of them—that meant Loomis had jarred Duke Ridge out of his indecision and convinced him the Salado Kid mustn't be allowed to get away. They were dimly visible as they hauled up as though debating where he had vanished. Pryor raised his gun, the butt plates hard in his fist, ready to defend himself if he must.

They had a problem, he thought. They wanted him, and they wanted him bad, but on the other hand more gunplay could draw too much attention. If their presence in Laredo tonight should become known, it could endanger all their plans for freeing Bart Campion.

Then the pair of them moved on out of sight, and Pryor lowered his revolver and let the hammer off cock. He forced some of the tightness from his shoulders, but he could not put out of his mind the disturbing things he had heard in that smoky kitchen.

As he holstered his gun and turned away, determined to put some distance between himself and the men who were hunting him, his only satisfaction was that Jim Dance had proved he could still be a friend, even if he wouldn't leave the gang and accept Pryor's offer of a partnership. But from this point on, he knew, if he met

Ridge or Loomis or any of the others that he'd once ridden with, it could only be as enemies—with no holds barred!

Chapter 10

Boyce Tuthill was concerned for Molly.

His feelings about her sharpened his perceptions as they watched Owen Pryor walk away from them to be swallowed up in the shadows of the trees that lined the plaza. He had an idea he knew what the girl was feeling: disappointment and hurt at the abrupt way she had been pushed off on another man without a word of explanation and abandoned there. His own curiosity about Pryor was swamped in resentment on her behalf—and, for himself, a stabbing pang of pure jealousy.

Her head was lowered so he could not see her face. He felt he had to say something. He asked, "Would you like to stay here a while longer? Or have you seen enough?"

"Oh . . ." She stirred herself. There was little of the usual animation in her voice as she answered. "It's been a very long day. We may as well start back."

"All right." He gave her a hand up, and they turned away from the music and from the pattern woven by the young people in their romantic ritual. The lights died behind them and the sound of the instruments gradually faded, and they were alone in the warm darkness of the Texas night.

Troubled by her silence, he said presently, "I hope you aren't still angry with me."

"What?" She seemed surprised at the question.

"For this afternoon. At the jail."

"Oh . . ."

When she said nothing more he blundered ahead, determined to try to set things right. "I'm afraid you got the wrong impression. I'd be lying to try to claim I'm not still as puzzled and curious as ever, but you mustn't think it's just because I'm a newspaperman looking for a story. Please believe I have no intention of prying into your affairs! On the other hand, I can't help but be concerned about you. Can I ask, at least, if you've decided how much longer you'll be staying in Laredo?"

"I've decided there's no point now in my being here at all," she said in a flattened tone. "I intend to leave in the morning—anyhow, on the first stage I can get."

That silenced him for a moment as they walked on through the darkness. "Then after tonight I may not be seeing you again. I'm sorry to hear it, and sorry things didn't go better for you. Truly I am."

A breeze had sprung up as the night grew older; it seemed to fan the stars to brighter light, making a rustling in dry leaves overhead as the last strains from the bandstand in Augustin Plaza were swallowed up behind them. The night was busy with sound. There was the racket from the saloons, and knots of men tramped the streets, their voices loud and raucous. Once they heard, unmistakably, a pair of gunshots that caused Molly to give an exclamation and draw closer to Tuthill. The shots were not repeated.

He said, "You see what's happening? Tomorrow's the big day, and this crowd in town has started on a drunken spree that will probably last all night unless the town marshal can get on top of things. The best anyone can do is keep out of sight and out of the way. We'll get you to your room, and then there's no reason anyone should bother you."

That reminded her of something. She said quickly, "I never even thought to ask—after all the trouble you went to for me: Did you find a place to stay, yourself?"

Tuthill laughed reassuringly. "Don't worry about that. It's never the same problem for a man." He saw no need to tell her that, having searched in vain for a room, he'd finally had to make arrangements to borrow a blanket from Will Perkins, the itinerant photographer, and to sleep on the ground beneath his wagon.

They brought the bulk of the courthouse into view now. Lamps burned in the sheriff's office and in the squat jail toward the rear. The finished gallows stood silhouetted against the stars. As they paused a moment they saw a man's dark shape move across one of the lamplit windows. In another part of the darkened square, a match sprang to light briefly as someone else fired up a cigarette.

Tuthill observed, "Swain doesn't appear to be taking any chances. For this last night, he's going to have every available man on guard duty, making sure nobody gets anywhere near his prisoner."

Molly said nothing. A vagrant gleam of light touched her face and showed her sober expression, and he couldn't help wondering at her thoughts, about the unnamed mission that she'd been unable to complete. He had to clamp his jaw to hold back the questions he had promised not to ask.

It was the girl who turned away finally. They started to walk the last few blocks to the Jackson house. Suddenly, almost without volition, he heard himself talking—telling her about a reporter's work, about himself and his ambitions.

"I'm proud of my profession," he told her almost defiantly. "Today, more than ever before, a newspaper has to serve as the eyes and ears for its readers. After all, these are the 1870s! It's not the same country it was back before the war—or before the railroad finished building and linked the oceans. Nowadays, to survive a man has to have his finger on the pulse of what's happening across the whole continent. Only the best reporting, in his daily paper, can make that possible. . . ." And so he continued with growing enthusiasm as he got into one of his favorite subjects, while the girl beside him gave no sign whether she was actually listening or was lost in thoughts of her own.

"I hope you realize," Tuthill went on earnestly, "I don't necessarily mean the story I'm working on now. A hanging isn't the kind of news I like to deal in—but they've turned this one into a circus, something people will insist on reading about. I'm not in a position yet to pick and choose my assignments. Starting out, you have to get your by-line in print whatever way you can. You never know which story may prove to be the big one for you—the breakthrough."

They turned the corner, and the Jackson house gleamed whitely in the darkness. As they halted, Molly turned to him. He looked at the pale oval of her face, and the knowledge that he was about to say good-bye for the last time to this brave and spunky girl drove him to unexpected lengths.

Speech poured from him. "Molly, I don't know how long it will take me, but sooner or later I intend to make good at this business! So far I'm a nobody—a stringer for a paper in a Missouri town that's hardly more than a frontier village. But they're not going to keep me down! I promise you I'm headed for bigger things—eventually, a job on a really important Eastern paper, maybe in Philadelphia or Boston or even New York City. You can take my word—it's going to happen!"

"I'm sure of it," Molly said as he paused for breath. He was suddenly appalled at what he felt must have sounded like empty boasting. But she appeared to be sincere, not at all put off by his manner. "If it's what you want . . . though personally—" She seemed to hesitate. "Maybe you wouldn't understand, but I really don't think I could ever be happy in one of those places. I suppose I'm just a country girl. Truth is, I wouldn't feel really comfortable in a town that was much bigger than—well, than this one."

"I see."

Boyce Tuthill thought he saw a lot. She had understood, all right, that in his own way he was proposing to her; and this was *her* way of refusing him, of gently letting him down. And she was right, of course. They were much too far apart, in temperament and attitudes. With his driving ambition and plans for the future there was simply no way he could be right for someone like her, and she at least had the sense to recognize it.

He was disappointed, of course, but he couldn't be angry. He nodded and drew a breath. "I see," he repeated. He took her hand then and held it as he said earnestly, "I guess this is good-bye, Molly. Whatever it is you do want, I hope you find it." He hoped there was no bitterness in his voice as he added, "I wonder, would it be a cattle ranch you're thinking about—say, over in New Mexico. . . ."

Molly Bishop was suddenly thankful for the darkness hiding the rush of warmth to her cheeks that made them feel all at once as though they were on fire. She tried to answer but only stammered, and then Boyce Tuthill released her hand and turned to stride away, leaving her there. She didn't think he had meant to embarrass her— he had proven many times that he respected her and intended her only the best. Still, he'd guessed the truth in a way that upset her as she watched the night swallow him up.

Had she really been so transparent? Had her interest in that strange man, Owen Pryor, been so obvious—and her feelings when he deserted her this evening in the plaza, with not even a lame excuse? At least Boyce Tuthill, who was a trained newspaper reporter and an astute observer, had seen through her without any trouble.

Well, she thought, there was nothing a person could do about the way she felt; even the hint of unspoken mystery about Owen Pryor, which had warned her against becoming emotionally involved with him, had been no deterrent to her emotions. If she were going to fall in love, why not with someone as fathomable and as guilelessly interested in herself as the man she had just now sent away? But though she had a genuine liking for Boyce Tuthill, she knew it couldn't ever come to anything more.

She shook her head in a futile gesture and turned toward the house. Her head jerked quickly as she saw something move in the shadows. Thinking of the men like Claib Meagher who thronged through the town tonight, she felt a stab of cold fear as she peered at the black mass of a bush growing beside the path. A bench was set beneath it, and she saw that someone had been waiting there. Now the figure got to its feet and at least it wasn't Meagher—not nearly big enough for that. But it alarmed her, all the same.

It didn't occur to her to call out or try to rouse the

Jacksons. The front of the house was dark, a faint glimmer of light showing through the open door which indicated someone might be at the back, in the kitchen perhaps. Thinking of the frail old man and woman, Molly felt it would be wrong to bring them into this even if she could.

She tried to keep a tremor from her voice as she demanded, "Who's there? What do you want?"

To her surprise, it was a woman's voice that answered her—rough-edged, but a woman's voice nonetheless. "Don't get all worked up, honey. I only want a word or two. I've been waiting here quite a spell."

"For me?" Surprised, but somehow no longer afraid, Molly Bishop moved closer. "I can't think why. I don't know you, do I? I don't know anybody here in Laredo."

"That's all right," the voice said. It was throaty, with a certain hoarse quality that Molly was sure she would have remembered had she ever heard it before now. "By this time, the whole town knows about *you*. There were plenty who saw you at the courthouse today and heard what you told that fool deputy sheriff. No way that kind of story will keep from spreading. When I heard it I only had to do some asking around to find out where you were staying."

Molly tried to peer through the shadows. "But, who *are* you? How can it be any concern of yours, what I might have done?"

"Anything to do with Bart Campion concerns me. And I want to know why you made such a fuss about getting in to see him."

"I didn't make a fuss!" Molly said indignantly. "I only asked—"

"You know what I mean!"

Someone went past the house with heavy tread of

boots. As Molly broke off, turning instinctively for a look, the woman's hand descended on her wrist, trapping it. She was pulled back into the shadows, and when she tried to jerk away found herself thrust down upon the bench. Leaning over her the woman said in a harsh whisper, "Look! I don't intend to hurt you any. But I mean to find out what I want to know!"

Molly managed to free her arm, but by now she was intrigued and made no effort to escape. The passerby had vanished, apparently without noticing anything. The woman seated herself and Molly rubbed her wrist as she peered at her.

She had an impression of a pale face beneath masses of dark hair and was aware of a rather strong perfume. She said with spirit, "Before I'll answer any questions, I expect you to tell me why it should be any business of yours."

"You want it flat out?" the other woman said crisply. "All right! I can only guess what your game is, young lady, but I don't like it! I haven't had a real good look at you, but you *sound* young—too young for the likes of Bart Campion. A hell of a lot too young for me to favor having you mixed up with him."

"What!" The exclamation was jarred from Molly, even as she thought she understood. "Oh, please! Surely you can't think that I—"

The other woman cut her off. "What I think is that I've been with Bart for a half-dozen years, and in all that time I never had a hint that he was seeing anyone else or that maybe he no longer figured me to be—"

Molly broke in, aghast: "But I assure you it's nothing like that! Because I've never so much as laid eyes on Bart Campion in my life!"

"I'm supposed to believe that?"

"It's the truth. I swear!"

After a long pause, the woman said in a tone that was still heavy with disbelief, "Well—we'll see! Maybe we better start over. Let's start with some names."

Molly quickly gave hers and in reply was told, "That's better! You can call me Cherry. The last name's Devore, if it matters to anybody."

"And you've really known Bart Campion as long as you say? Six years?" All at once Molly was beginning to tremble a little. "Then you must know quite a lot about him—things he might have told you about his past. From before the war, even . . ."

"That's quite a ways back," Cherry Devore remarked. "Say—what's on your mind? What is it you're trying to ask me?"

That was all the encouragement Molly needed. With no more prompting than that, she poured out her story. She could almost feel the woman's stare pinned on her through the gloom of night that concealed their faces. Having already unburdened herself to Owen Pryor made it easier to do so this time, especially now when there seemed a chance she might be about to learn something in answer to her agonizing questions. But when she finished, there was nothing for a long moment. Finally Cherry Devore broke the stillness with a question of her own. "And what was this girl's name? Your mother, I mean . . ."

"Lorena. Lorena Wakeman. She died two years ago."

"I see." But then Molly's hopes were dashed as she was told, "Sorry, but I can't help you any. Naturally I never figured I was Bart's first woman, but he's had the good sense never to brag to me about the others. He knew better than that!"

"Then—there's nothing at all you can tell me?"

"I never heard mention from him of any Lorena, or any Wakeman either. Before the war, you said." Her voice, coming out of that dimly seen blur of a face, took on an edge of pure bitterness. "Honey, far as I'm concerned anything that happened before the war is ancient history, best forgotten. It's no matter now, and sure as hell nothing's going to bring it back!" Listening to her, Molly heard some echo in her words of this woman's own lost past, of a better time destroyed and irretrievably vanished. It was something she could only guess at, however, for there was no attempt to elaborate on it.

"At least," Molly said, "perhaps now you understand why I wanted so much to see Bart Campion."

"And maybe *you* can see why I jumped to conclusions. I didn't mean to give you a bad time. Sorry." The woman laid her hand on Molly's and gave it a brief pat, then as quickly removed it. She added, "No, I can't say if Bart was your old man or not. But I'm not sure how much pleasure it would give you to find out he was!"

"Why do you say that?" Molly exclaimed. "What is he like? Please—tell me something about him."

If anyone could, surely this woman who was his mistress should be the one, but Cherry Devore hesitated before she answered with plain reluctance, "About all I can say is that over the past year or so, he's—changed. He's changed a lot. I hardly think I know him anymore. . . ." Some emotion brought her suddenly to her feet. "Look, I've done all the talking I can right now. I—I feel like I'm pretty near out of my head!"

Molly rose quickly. This time she was the one who put out a sympathetic hand. She laid it on the woman's arm and felt her shaking, and not with cold—the evening was warm. She said earnestly, "I'm sorry. I honestly am!"

"I been here in Laredo all these weeks," the Devore woman said miserably. "All during the trial and afterwards. Just to be as near him as I could—knowing there isn't a damn thing I can *do* . . ."

Hesitantly, Molly suggested, "Do you suppose there's a chance something might—happen? What about all the talk that his gang may be in the neighborhood?"

"Oh, yes!" Her voice was bitter. "Bart's gang! They're here, all right. I've seen 'em around, and I've had words with one or two. Sure, they've got ideas. But I know that bunch! I've known them too long. On their own, without Bart planning every move—I just couldn't say what they'll do. Play hell, more than likely! But get him free? . . .

"You know, it's pretty strange—you asking me that," she went on. "When I seen you with one of the old crowd just this very evening."

"Me!" Molly could only stare. "Oh, you're mistaken! How could I know any of them? If you mean that young man who brought me home just now—why, he's a newspaper reporter. From Kansas City."

The woman shook her head impatiently. "No, no— not him. Not that dude! I mean earlier. I was watching from across the street there, and I seen this fellow come up to the door. And afterwards you left with him and started off toward the river."

It was as though a cold hand had begun to squeeze off Molly's breath. Suddenly, all the unanswered questions about Owen Pryor rushed in upon her: the sense of an unrevealed past, the unstated reason for his being here in Laredo and for suddenly abandoning her there at the plaza—the many half-hints that were never fully explained. But she found her voice, to exclaim, "Oh, I know that can't be right!"

"Don't tell *me* it can't. It's been a while, and he's grown a mustache, but I had a real good look and I'd have known him anywhere. Oh, he was in the gang, all right. The Salado Kid, we used to call him." A piercing look sought Molly's eyes in the darkness. "You mean, he didn't *tell* you that? Well, then all I got to say is—you better watch your step with him!"

Moments later the woman was gone, her figure erect and head held high, her footsteps fading as the night swallowed her up. Molly Bishop was left with a feeling that all that was sure and true in her world had crashed down about her where she stood.

Chapter 11

Jim Dance, a man with problems, had had a restless night because of them. Almost as soon as he got to sleep, the ear-splitting crow of a rooster under his window brought him groaning to wakefulness. He lay a moment staring at the ceiling, rubbing a palm across the rasp of beard stubble on his cheeks. Early morning laid a square of light from the window crookedly athwart one corner of the room. Heat was already building. And then, remembering what day this was, he groaned again. With no more sleep in him, he levered himself up from the crude hay-filled mattress.

His clothes were flung carelessly on a chair, his cartridge belt and revolver hanging from the back of it. He got himself dressed, buckled the gun in place, and picked up his boots. He stood a moment looking down at Conchita where she lay face down, still asleep, long black hair spread across her brown and naked shoulders. Carrying the boots so as not to awaken her, he padded across the dirt floor in his stocking feet and into the other room, drawing the door closed behind him.

The odors of yesterday's cooking lay heavy in the stale air of the kitchen. Dance took a whiskey bottle from the table, held it up, and seeing it was empty set it down again. Maybe some coffee, then. He ran his tongue over his teeth as he looked for the soot-blackened pot and found it sitting in the ashes of the fireplace. He went over and got it, shook it, and looked inside. It didn't look promising; he would have to make fresh. But first, he had business at the outhouse. He stomped into his boots and stepped out the rear door into the fresher air of morning.

The rooster crowed again and was answered by others here and there across the town. Smoke from morning cook fires already stood in wavering pencil strokes above mud chimneys, reaching toward a cloudless sky, and the tang of burning piñon chunks blended with the strong, dark scent of the river. At the rear of the lot some past owner had built a horse shed large enough to hold a couple of animals. When Dance had finished at the outhouse and was returning to the shack, the sound of a shod hoof striking against a timber drew his attention to the shed, where he had left his black gelding the evening before. At another stomp and a whicker, he swore a little—that horse had a nervous temperament and it sounded as though some varmint might have got into the shed and was disturbing it. So he changed his course and went tramping over there to find out.

He reached the structure and put a hand on the door latch, listening. There was no further sound and he decided he was probably mistaken; nevertheless he half-drew his gun as he pushed the door inward on its leather hinges.

There were no windows and it was dark in there, except for strips of thin daylight where the carelessly nailed boards failed to overlap. He saw the black but could detect nothing amiss until the horse moved slightly and a finger of light gleamed across the big, silver pommel

111

of the charro saddle on its back. He stiffened, his eyes narrowing. He had stripped the gear from his animal when he put it in here last night, yet now the saddle was back in place, one cinch strap dangling, and the silver-studded halter had been fitted over the black's head. It was only then, as his eyes adjusted to the deceptive, light-banded gloom, he caught sight of a second horse, one that had no business being there at all.

Next moment a boot scraped the dirt and Owen Pryor eased into view from the darker shadows. "Come on in, Jim," he said quietly.

Dance stepped across the low sill, moving carefully. "Kid! What the hell are you doing here?"

"Saddling your horse," Pryor answered. "He doesn't like it." Even as he spoke, the black, reacting to the unfamiliar voice, stomped and moved uneasily, and again a hoof struck hollowly against the wall behind it. "I'd intended coming for you in the house," Pryor continued, "but you've saved me the trouble. You and I," he explained, "are about to take a ride."

"No we ain't!" Dance snapped.

With no change of expression Pryor lifted a hand into view and there was a sixshooter in it, leveled at Dance across the saddle of the black. He said, "You'll come with me, Jim. And you won't make any trouble."

Dance stared at the gun. "Or you'll use that thing on me?" He shook his head and managed a grin, saying, "Now, you know you couldn't do that to an old friend! Have you forgotten? You said yourself, I'm the fellow that saved your life!"

"I haven't forgotten. It's the only reason I came here this morning." Pryor moved toward the other man, squeezing in front of the black and causing it to toss its

112

head nervously. Keeping Dance covered, he slipped the latter's gun from the holster and shoved it behind his waistband. He said, "You might as well understand this: I'm here to see that, whatever happens in this town today, at noon—you're not going to have any part in it! If I have to wing you, I will."

Dance felt the heat rise into his cheeks. "Damn it, you can't do that! I got—!"

"We'll argue it later." Pryor gestured with the gun muzzle. "Finish doing up that cinch and let's get out of here. . . ."

He started to turn away. That was a mistake. Dance, seeing him off guard, lashed out suddenly and his fist took Pryor on the side of the head just above the ear. He was flung off balance, so that he fell against the flimsy boards hard enough to cause the whole wall to tremble. He lost his gun, the back of his fist striking the hard edge of an upright, the weapon squirting out of his fingers to drop into the dirt. Immediately, Dance was after him.

He closed the distance with fists swinging and caught Pryor in the ribs and grazed a blow along his cheekbone. But then the other man managed to get a body hold on him, trapping his arms. He pushed off the wall and wrestled Dance backward across the crowded space of the shed amid dust that rose under scuffling boots and into the streaks of daylight falling through the cracks between the boards. The skittish black gave a squeal and tried to sidle away from the violence. It only crowded against Pryor's animal, which added to the disturbance as it tried to nip at the black's shoulder with strong yellow teeth, and an iron-shod hoof struck one of the sun-dried timbers and split it with a report like a pistol shot.

Abruptly, the fight ended when Pryor hurled Dance

backward, and he struck the ground on his shoulders. Winded, he looked up to see the other man standing over him, with Dance's own revolver leveled at him.

Pryor said in a harsh voice that the outlaw had never heard from him, "You're going with me. In the saddle straight up, or tied face down across it. It's your pick!"

Dance, sprawled on the hard dirt, peered up at the angry face above him. He said, "You sonofabitch."

Pryor picked up his own gun from where it had fallen, blew down the barrel to dislodge any loose dirt, and shoved the weapon into his holster. He had lost his hat in the scuffle and he picked it up and drew it on. "All right," he said. "Get up from there."

Jim Dance looked into the black muzzle of the revolver pointed at him. "You seem to have made up my mind for me."

Pryor watched without speaking as he got to his feet. Dance approached the black, said a few words to settle it, and then got the dangling cinch strap and finished the interrupted job of lashing the saddle into place. As soon as the man was ready, Pryor pulled the door open and motioned for his prisoner to leave first, following afterward with his own chestnut gelding on the reins. Outside, they mounted up.

Dance cast a look toward the rear of the house; there, in the doorway, Conchita stood with a dirty wrapper carelessly pulled about her, her long black hair lying uncombed to her shoulders. Likely the commotion in the horse shed had wakened her. Now she stared at them across the barren yard as though trying to fathom what might be happening.

Owen Pryor spoke. "Never mind about her. Just ride up the alley. I'll be right behind you."

Dance grunted sourly. He gave the reins a tug that moved the black around, its head tossing and hoofs scraping up the dirt. They rode past the shed and put the house from sight behind them.

They pointed their animals north at a walk, threading the littered back streets of Laredo, picking a course Pryor thought would take them through the town without attracting notice. After the last building fell away he kept a look back, watching for any stain of dust or other sign that they were being followed. He could see none. The morning grew older, a molten sun rose up into a sky free of clouds, and the earth began to shimmer with heat waves. The twin ruts of the stage road rolled back beneath their horses' hoofs as Pryor set a steady gait.

Once, out of a brooding silence, Jim Dance spoke up demanding, "Where are we headed? Maybe you figure to drag me clear to New Mexico with you?"

Owen Pryor shook his head. "I just wish I thought that would do any good. I'd like to believe you'd decided that going back to wrangling cattle wasn't such a bad idea after all."

"We've been all over that," Dance said shortly. "Nothing's happened to change my mind."

"I didn't suppose so."

"Then where the hell *are* you taking me?"

But he got no answer.

Owen Pryor kept pushing hard, aware of the passing of time. He stayed with the stage road because it made easy going, but finally left it for a shorter course through the chaparral and broken land. Morning drew on. The sun was well up when they brought the abandoned desert jacal at last into sight—the broken corrals, the well, and the adobe building that seemed ready to sink back into the earth. There was no sign of life here, no sound except the strong hot wind tearing at encroaching brush. They quartered in on the place and halted. Looking around, Jim Dance wanted to know, "What the hell place is this?"

"I happened to stumble onto it yesterday," Pryor told him. "It's just what it looks like—a starve-out spread with a well that went dry." He added, "Get down."

He was already dismounting. Dance seemed on the verge of balking but swung off and stood scowling, watching as the other man tied both horses to a corral post. Pryor had stowed the prisoner's captured gun in a pocket of his saddlebags; now he took down a coil of rope he had carried lashed to the horn string, and looking at Dance he nodded toward the door of the shack. "Inside," he ordered.

Dance stiffened. "What happens then?" But Pryor merely looked at him, and he let himself be marched over to the building and inside. The bottom of the sagging plank door scraped the dirt as it was forced open, and Pryor shut it again, then dropped the latch into place. Jim Dance was staring with angry suspicion around the single dirt-floored room, empty except for the broken table. Through the opening of the smashed windows came smells of warm earth and of the sun-heated chaparral that grew, like a jungle, almost up to the walls of the ruined house.

"Turn around," Pryor ordered crisply. "And put your hands behind you."

They stood confronted in that hot stillness, their faces shadowed and beaded with sweat. Dance showed his wish to rebel, but again something in Pryor's eyes, or perhaps the set of his features, changed his mind. He swore under his breath and then did as he was commanded. At once a noose was slipped over his wrists and jerked tight, and quick flips of the rope pinioned his arms. That done, Pryor shoved him into a corner and made him sit there. It took only moments to finish the job by tying the prisoner's ankles securely, after which Pryor settled back on his heels.

Dance had papers and a tobacco sack in his vest pocket. Pryor took them out and shook rough cut into a paper. Having returned the makings he began to shape a cigarette as he said, "I don't enjoy this business any more than you do. But you didn't give me any choice."

The prisoner glared at him. He had been testing the ropes, pulling at the knots that held him fast. He gave that up and said coldly, "It ain't too hard to guess what this is all about! You've been to the courthouse, I suppose—to warn them."

"No," Pryor told him. "I'm not even sure but that Harry Swain would rather throw me in jail than listen to anything I could tell him. And before I did anything I had to make sure first that you'd be safely out of it."

Anger swelled the prisoner's chest. "And did you figure I'd *thank* you for making me sit here helpless, while I know you're betraying the rest of the gang?" He added bitterly, "Especially when it was me insisted Loomis was wrong by saying we couldn't trust you!"

His eyes on what his hands were doing, Owen Pryor said, "I've never been partial to traitors. But don't forget that after I left you last evening Loomis and Ridge came after me. They intended to kill me without bothering to see *what* I might have had in mind. And if the light had been better they would have finished me off!

"By my reckoning, what they did cancels any loyalty I owed that outfit. Even so I don't take lightly what I have to do. But I've fought it out with myself, and I've decided there's no way I can stand by and let them shoot down people at random in that courthouse square today."

Jim Dance frowned. "All right. Maybe I ain't too crazy about that part of it myself. But it's the only idea anyone came up with that has a chance of working. And what's the difference, anyway? You must have seen the scum that's been pouring into Laredo! They think watching a man die on a rope is some kind of circus. Who gives a damn if some of them should get it instead?"

Pondering his answer, Pryor deliberately finished shaping the cigarette. He licked the tab and pressed it down. "That's easy to say—if you forget that most of those men have got women and kids somewhere. How about *them?* That's what I'm chiefly thinking about. That's why I've got to try and prevent it."

He pinched off the ends of the cigarette and put it between the other man's lips. Dance promptly spat it out again. "And what about Bart?" he exclaimed angrily. "Don't *he* count? Don't you care a damn if he hangs?"

"Very well." Pryor spoke with deliberation. "So, what about Bart Campion? I knew a man by that name once. He was a hard man but I think he tried to be a fair one. At the age I was when I joined the outfit, I admired and pretty much respected him. But I've never considered I was under any particular obligations. I simply followed his orders—and they ended up getting me two years in prison!

"Jim, I don't even *know* the man sitting in that jail at Laredo! The Bart Campion I remember would never have hunted down a man who had been his friend or lay an ambush and murder him right in front of his wife! To me that sounds insane. And if that's what he's become, I'm

118

not sure he's worth saving. Not at the expense of a lot of other people, even the kind who'll be crowding into that courthouse square in another hour or so for the sport of seeing him hang!"

He looked to Dance for an answer but got none, nor could he read any change at all in the man's heavy scowl. Pryor gave a shrug and pushed up to his feet. "Anyway, I guess you know now what I have to try and do. Time's getting too short to argue it with you. I have to go. And don't worry—if something happens that I don't make it back, you'll be all right. I've tied those knots loose enough. You should be able to work out of them in time. I'll leave your horse. Though you've made up your mind against throwing in with me, I at least hope you'll decide to get on him and ride clear away from Laredo and whatever is left of the gang."

"What you mean is go back to cowboying!" Dance said scornfully.

"What I mean is there can be only one end to the road you're on now. Bart Campion's reached it. You can do better, if you want—before it's too late! Remember, Jim, I've tried both roads. I know what I'm saying."

But words were having no effect on Dance. With a shake of the head Pryor turned away from the unswerving hostility in the face of his prisoner. He was at the door and his hand was on the latch when outside he heard the nervous whicker of a horse.

Reacting to the sound, thinking something might have got at the mounts they had left tied to the corral post, he was drawing his gun as he dragged the door open. Sunlight was a dazzle after the gloom of the ruined shack. He could see no sign of trouble, but he had to take a couple of steps into the open in order to get a good view of the corral. As he did a voice spoke, just to his right: "There's a gun aimed at you, Kid. Let's see yours on the ground!"

He froze and slowly turned his head. Duke Ridge stood just at the corner of the building, and Pryor had walked right into his sights. He looked at the sixshooter pointed at him, and he looked into the other man's face. He knew he had no choice but to obey. He bent and gingerly laid his own weapon in the dirt and, at a command from Ridge, gave it a nudge with his boot that sent it sliding over in the outlaw's direction.

Pryor said heavily, "How did you find me?"

"Easy," Ridge told him. "You couldn't have been gone long when Loomis and I arrived at Conchita's looking for Jim, and she told us you'd tooken off with him. I set out to pick up your trail, while Loomis went and fetched a couple of the boys from camp. Esteban, there, is some kind of a tracker—he led us right to you."

Ridge indicated the trio approaching from the direction of the corrals. Esteban would be the lean Mexican youth with the drooping left eyelid; he, Merl Loomis, and the third man all carried guns, and now Loomis demanded harshly, "All right, Kid! What have you done with him?"

In answer, Jim Dance's shout came from within the ruined adobe: "Hey! Somebody come in and cut me loose!"

Loomis swore. He told the others, "I'll do it," and gave Pryor a malevolent glare as he shoved past him and strode inside the building. The rest, waiting, heard muffled voices. In a few minutes Jim Dance emerged, ducking the low lintel. He was shaking off the ropes that

had held him pinioned and rubbing his chafèd wrists.
Loomis followed, knife in hand. He told them, "Damned
if he wasn't trussed up like a hog ready for the butcher!"

They were all looking at Dance. When he came
abreast of Pryor he stopped and stood glaring at the man
who had been his friend. His hands balled into fists, and
Pryor braced himself, expecting Dance to take a swing at
him. But the other turned away as Duke Ridge demanded,
"Speak up, Jim! What the hell was he after?"

Slowly the tension ran out of Dance's shoulders; his
expression altered. He said with a shrug, "Does it matter?
Time is short. Let me fetch my gun out of his saddlebag,
and then we better start for town."

"Oh, no!" Merl Loomis snapped the blade of his
clasp knife into the handle and dropped it into a pocket of
his jeans. He had holstered his gun. Now he started to
draw it again as he looked at Pryor. "We ain't finished
here yet! I told you last night this fellow was poison. Now
I want to know what other surprises he's got planned. A
trap, I'll wager, all set and waiting for us at the courthouse.
You gonna deny it, Kid?" The gun was in his hand, the
barrel raised threateningly. "Tell the truth, damn you, if
you don't want me to bust your face!"

Pryor eyed the gun barrel, poised as though ready to
smash him. He heard an indistinct sound of protest from
Duke Ridge. But it was Jim Dance who seized Loomis by
a shoulder, crying out, "Lay off him! There isn't any
trap!"

Loomis shook off his hand. "And how would you
know?"

"Because he told me!" At the other's scornful sneer,
Dance's face reddened with anger. "Damn it, he did! He
brought me out here and tied me up because he said he

121

didn't want me involved. Only *then* he was going to the sheriff's office. . . ."

He broke off as though realizing that in his anxiety to persuade he had blurted too much and signed his friend's death warrant.

"He said that, did he?" Loomis exclaimed, and as he turned again to Pryor the latter read what was written in the man's hot stare. He didn't wait. He had one chance; he caught at the hand that held the raised revolver—missed, grabbed the man's sleeve instead. Loomis swore and jerked free, but for an instant he was off balance and desperately Pryor gave a shove that hurled him toward Duke Ridge.

Ridge tried to step aside but Loomis stumbled into him, his boots tangling under him. Somebody cried out in surprise. Taking advantage of the confusion, Pryor swung away, trying for the open door of the house just behind him. He collided with the edge of the jamb but recovered and plunged through, grabbing the door and dragging it shut behind him. Even as the latch fell there was the sound of a shot, and a sudden line of sunlight sprang through a hole punched into the wood. Pryor leaped away from the door; the bullet kicked up a glitter of dust where it struck the adobe of the opposite wall.

Angry voices shouted. Instantly bullets began eating into the flimsy panel and hitting the front wall of the shack. Unarmed as he was, Pryor knew this place was no shelter. In another minute they'd be circling the hovel to shoot at him through the broken windows. He saw only one escape, and with the thought he was already in motion. The window in the wall opposite the door was none too large, but he went through it in a dive. He landed on hard ground and was up at once, heading for the brush.

He plunged into it, dodging the spiny thorns that caught at his clothing. Behind him, the guns had stopped their banging; his enemies would have given up their futile attempt to shoot that door off its hinges. Once they came around the shack, hunting a window, and sighted him, he would be little better off than when he was trapped inside. But now he saw the mouth of a dry wash just ahead of him. He took a blind leap. Loose earth crumbled and spilled down with him as he went over the edge, rolling onto his hands and knees on the stony ground at the bottom. He crouched there catching his breath and listening for the yells that would indicate he'd been discovered.

He heard nothing at first except a buzz of insects and a rattling of the hot wind in thorny scrub. Then voices sounded. They were angry and excited voices that tumbled over one another so that Pryor couldn't make out what they said. But the loud tones of Duke Ridge overrode the others: "Wherever he is, he can't do us any damage now—not on foot in that bush. We haven't got the time to bother with him. Let him go."

"Nothing doing!" That was Merl Loomis, almost raging in his fury at the prisoner's escape. "I ain't leaving here till I see that turncoat get what he has coming! Somebody fetch up the horses—if we spread out, it can't take too long!"

Horses! In this scatter of chaparral, a man afoot and without weapons could have little show against armed riders determined to chase him down. For just a moment Pryor thought about his own animal, tied at the corral, but he quickly gave up the idea of trying to circle and reach it. They'd have thought of that too, and with five men they could spare a guard to keep an eye on the chestnut in case he might make such a play.

Instead, Pryor came up to his feet and started at a run along the bottom of the arroyo, deeper into the brush. Though it was floored with rock and litter that should take few prints, he couldn't let himself forget what Duke Ridge had said about one of the outlaws being a tracker. That was bad luck! Without a gun, his one chance lay in finding a place where he could hole up and hope the pressure to get back to Laredo before the hanging would finally force his enemies to give up and call off their manhunt.

The draw twisted and deepened. Loose silt dragged at Pryor's boots, and the dry heat that collected and concentrated in the motionless air along the arroyo bottom already had the sweat streaming. It was as he paused a moment to listen that he felt in the ground, rather than heard, a thud of nearing hoofbeats that warned him a rider was approaching. He came on at a good clip. Very soon Pryor could hear the grunting of the horse and a swish of brush against saddle fenders. Whoever he was, the rider must be making straight toward him.

He was trapped, with no place down here to hide. At the last moment Pryor did the only thing he could. He threw himself to a crouch against the wall of the arroyo on the off chance a rider on the flat above him might not look closely enough to see him there. And then he stiffened in sudden horror at a new sound that made cold sweat break out.

The rattlesnake had been shading under the protection of a clump of scrub, barely a yard from where he landed on hands and knees. Startled, it had reared and the cruel eyes were pinned on him, while a darting tongue tested for his scent and rattles buzzed in an angry blur. Pryor went rigid, stomach churning with fear. There'd been no time for the snake to coil but he knew that made no difference—the reptile could still strike. His empty holster mocked him. A hasty glance failed to discover anything within reach that he could use as a missile.

He gathered himself, fighting the primitive terror that slackened his muscles as he considered risking a sudden lunge backward and away from those deadly fangs.

And at that instant the flat, triangular head vanished in a mist of blood as a pistol shot sounded just above the spot where Pryor crouched. He stared at the snake's body that was jerked and flung lifeless by the bullet; only then did he manage to break free of his paralysis and, twisting about, gaze straight up the arroyo's crumbling side.

At the edge of the drop, Dance was bringing his nervous horse under control. Smoke still leaked from the muzzle of the gun which—for a second time now—had saved Owen Pryor from the strike of a rattler. From the saddle, he returned Pryor's look, but if his face held any emotion it was unreadable. And now the gun barrel moved in the outlaw's hand and came to a deliberate rest in line with Owen Pryor's head. For a long moment their glances locked. There was no sound except for the blowing of the black horse and a pop of saddle leather as the animal moved restlessly under its rider.

Slowly the gun barrel lowered. Still without expression, Jim Dance let the weapon drop into his holster. An abrupt jerk of the reins pulled the black's head around, and Dance rode off the arroyo rim. Where he had been was nothing but sun-filled, eye-punishing sky. Owen Pryor was left staring after him, with the headless snake still jerking its life out beside him in the sand.

Chapter 12

The sun was climbing higher. The riders, scattering as they pushed their horses through the brush in search of the fugitive, were dwarfed by the immensity of sky and encircling chaparral. Duke Ridge and Merl Loomis had come together for a brief discussion, and they looked around as Dance spurred toward them.

Anticipating the moments just ahead, Dance's breathing was tight and his mouth felt dry. Ridge might not be too bright, but he knew Merl Loomis for a suspicious and dangerous fellow—he was the one it would be hard to fool. Dance kept his face a mask, and as he rode up he called, "It's all right, boys, I got the sonofabitch!"

He made as though he would ride on, but Loomis demanded harshly, "What the hell did you say?"

Jim Dance reined in the black, half-turning in feigned impatience. "I said, I got him. I'm surprised you never heard the shot."

"We heard one," Duke Ridge agreed. "Are you telling us you found the Kid? You *killed* him?"

Dance nodded, whereupon Merl Loomis wanted to know, "Then, where is he?"

"Back yonder." Dance made a vague gesture. "I left him lying in a gully."

"I suppose you're sure he's dead?"

That got Loomis a cold stare and a scornful answer that Jim Dance hoped would sound convincing. "If you could see what's left of his face, you wouldn't have to ask! I wasn't taking any chances with him, not after the trick he played on me this morning."

"So you tell us." Merl Loomis's scowl was dark with suspicion. "You and the Kid used to be pretty thick. How do we know you're giving this to us straight?"

"You calling me a liar?" Jim Dance made himself face the other man squarely and put everything into a bluff. "Come along if you want to see for yourself. Though I told you, he's not much to look at." He spurred past Loomis and then turned impatiently, his expression boldly insolent. "Well? You coming?"

He waited, while sweat streamed under the boil of the sun and a fly droned lazily in the stillness. For a moment he thought the bluff had worked—he hadn't even let himself think what he would do if Loomis called his hand and insisted on being shown Pryor's body. Then a knot, like a doubled fist, tightened in Dance as the outlaw said, "Hell, yes! I'm right behind you!" and gave his horse a kick.

But Duke Ridge intervened. "No!" he exclaimed sharply. "Lay off, you two! Can't you see the sun? It'll be noon, and us still sitting here, arguing about nothing! We'll take Jim's word." Not allowing an argument he turned and jerked out his gun, pointed it skyward, and let off three shots, a signal. Across the sun-struck stretch of chaparral, two riders turned and Ridge, holstering the weapon, took off his sweated hat and swung it in a circle, waving them in. "Come on!" he shouted. "We're needed in town. . . ."

As he reined away, his manner carried enough authority that even the scowling Merl Loomis was towed along, reluctantly, in his wake. Dance kept his face expressionless, but trapped breath left him in a shaky sigh of relief.

There would have been real trouble had these men learned of the way he deliberately let Owen Pryor go, untouched, and then lied to them about it. Yet in that moment when he sat his saddle at the edge of the wash, with the Salado Kid below him and helpless under his gun, he had known there was no choice.

He had done a thing he had to do. When you came down to it, friendship didn't allow room for debate.

Anybody who knew him might have guessed the pressure growing on Duke Ridge. It showed in the way he rode, with his shoulders hunched and his head shot forward, his heavy brows knotted in a baffled scowl. The sun stood almost overhead, uncomfortably close to noon. They had lost too much time, and he kept urging the others for speed. When Loomis lagged and then brought his knot-headed roan gelding to a halt, Ridge pulled rein and turned back, all but shouting, "What the hell is the matter *now?*"

"It's the roan," Loomis said. "I think he's coming up lame." And while Ridge swore at the delay, he deliberately swung down to have a look. He lifted his mount's off foreleg, examined the hoof, set it down again, and ran a probing hand over the corded muscle. His mouth pursed up and his eyes narrowed in concentration.

Ridge said impatiently, "Animal looks all right to me."

"But he ain't." The man straightened. He said flatly, "I won't ride him like this. It could ruin him."

Duke Ridge swore again while the others waited. It was Jim Dance who offered a suggestion. The reins of

Owen Pryor's chestnut—still carrying Pryor's saddle and gear—were anchored to his pommel; he unhooked them and held them out to Loomis, saying, "Here—take the Kid's animal. You can lead the roan."

Loomis hesitated. Roweled by impatience, Ridge made a gesture with one flat palm. "Do it, man—do it!" he snapped. "And let's *go!*"

With a shrug, Loomis stepped to accept the reins Jim Dance passed down to him. But instead of mounting he said, "First I got to check that leg some more. Don't let me hold the rest of you back. I'll catch up."

Duke Ridge didn't like it, though he didn't argue. "All right—but, hurry! We don't want to have to start the show without you."

For only a moment Dance hung back, a speculative frown resting on Loomis. The latter was already turning again to the horse that had gone lame, examining the hurt leg with a skilled horseman's attention. Dance's look remained thoughtful, but he gave his animal a kick that sent it off down the stage road after Ridge and the others.

Merl Loomis set down the roan's hoof and slowly straightened, looking after the disappearing riders. When a dip in the land and a clump of dusty trees swallowed them from view, the dust settling and silence returning, he gave a grunt of satisfaction and at once became all business. The horse Dance had turned over to him would be a nuisance, and for a moment he considered casting it loose, then instead he anchored its reins to a sturdy mesquite clump to hold it there until he returned for it. Quickly then he swung back onto his own saddle and turned the roan, giving it the spur to send it at a sharp clip back again toward the ruins of the deserted ranch.

The roan responded to the spur, showing no sign at all of being threatened with lameness.

Owen Pryor came out of the brush warily. It was hard enough to believe that moment back there in the arroyo, when he had looked up into the smoking muzzle of Jim Dance's revolver and then had seen Dance turn and deliberately ride away. Sometime after that, there had been three spaced gunshots, like a signal calling the searchers in, and then he had heard nothing at all. Finally he was forced to believe the hunt was over and he was alone.

Now the back of the crumbling house rose ahead of him. He approached cautiously, gained a rear corner, and worked forward to where he could look into the yard. He was not too surprised to find it lying empty and silent under the brassy sun. He saw the outlaws had even taken his own chestnut gelding from the broken corral fence where he had tied it. So he was stranded here, as little danger to them as if they had actually managed to track him down and kill him.

Standing there engulfed by the hot sunlight bouncing off the crumbling adobe wall at his back, he knew a mood of angry futility.

He remembered the gun Duke Ridge had forced him to discard, and he walked out into the open to look for it. But though he searched about the open space of hardpan, marked now with boot tracks and the prints of horses, there was no sign of the weapon. The outlaws hadn't been careless enough to leave it for him. One thing he did find lying in the dust was the rope Merl Loomis had cut to set Jim Dance free. It had been a good rope, a new one, and without thinking much about it Pryor picked it up. Loomis had used his knife freely but there was still a good length intact. Coiling it gave Pryor's hands something to do while his brain worked on thoughts that didn't come to anything.

He remembered that he was no more than a couple of miles from the stage trace. It looked as if his only choice was to walk over there and wait for a coach or a wagon to come by eventually and pick him up. In any case, he might as well forget whatever idea he'd had about interceding in the events soon to take place at Laredo. He could see no way at all now of getting there in time.

It was then that he heard the first sounds of a rider rapidly approaching.

An instinct for caution took him the few paces to the old well to drop on one knee behind it while he looked out over the rangeland. The hoofbeats stitched echoes across a stretch of hard rock, then a mounted figure broke suddenly into view among the scrub growth, coming from the south on a line directly toward the ranch.

When he recognized the spare figure of Merl Loomis—the man's stiff, straight-up way of sitting the leather—at first he didn't believe it. Suddenly he swore under his breath. This well coping was no protection. He couldn't be caught in the open without any way to defend himself. When he saw the rider vanish briefly into a swale, Pryor seized his chance; he was up at once and heading for the house. He didn't enter but instead ducked around the corner of it and there flattened himself in position where he could look into the yard. He waited.

Loomis topped into sight again, near enough this time for Pryor to make out the man's features. He was coming more slowly now and at last drew up to a halt. In that moment it was quiet enough for Pryor to hear distinctly the animal's breathing and the creak of saddle leather. The outlaw had the reins in his left hand and now he drew his belt gun with his right. His restless glance prowled the yard.

Pryor's jaw went hard. He knew beyond any doubt just why Loomis had returned.

Apparently satisfied he wouldn't find what he wanted here, Loomis spurred his animal forward to ride past the house toward the chaparral that lay beyond it. Anticipating this move Pryor had already faded back toward the rear of the building. He waited there out of sight, and as he heard the rider cantering nearer he took the length of rope from his shoulder.

He had only moments, but his hands worked swiftly, expertly fashioning a loop to replace the one Loomis's knife had ruined. He jerked the slipknot tight as Loomis came in view past the rear corner of the house; Pryor let him go by and then stepped swiftly forward, shaking out his loop. There wasn't time to make a proper cast. He simply circled it once about his head and then let fly—and as luck would have it, at that moment the roan sidestepped, spoiling his target. Instead of settling into place, the loop slapped the rider's shoulder and fell harmlessly away. Loomis jerked around, saw Pryor, and gave a shout of triumph as he reined about and kicked with the spur. The roan came barreling straight at Pryor, who was snatching in the rope. The gun rose in Loomis's fist. Pryor leaped aside as the gun spoke but missed. Then the horse was upon him, pounding past so close that a sweat-streaked shoulder almost knocked him flat.

Pryor used the only weapon he had. He flung up the coil of rope and struck out with it.

The coils slapped hard against the mounted man's shoulder and chest and trapped the hand that held his gun. To the forward leap of the horse under him, Loomis's arm was jerked around and the gun sprang out of his fingers; he barely managed to keep from being unseated. And Pryor, dropping the rope, turned to retrieve the revolver where it had fallen into the dirt.

It was still smoking from the shot that narrowly missed him. He grabbed it up, turning—and saw that Merl Loomis had a spare. The outlaw had reined about and the second gun was already in his hand; he slanted the barrel down and fired a split second before Pryor could find the trigger.

The two guns spoke almost together, the sounds mingling and carried away on the ground wind that scattered powder smoke and dust. The frightened horse lunged on, and Pryor found he was still on his feet—but Merl Loomis lay sprawled upon his back where a bullet in the chest had dumped him. The man was dead. The hideout gun he'd tried to use on Pryor lay beside him, and Pryor picked it up; the weapon was his own. He slid it into the holster.

Staring at the outlaw's slack features, Pryor said aloud, "Old hatreds die hard."

Now he was rearmed, with Loomis's horse nearby on dragging reins. The sun stood nearly overhead. For all he knew it was already too late for him to get back to Laredo in time. But Pryor started for the roan as the animal tossed its head and moved away from him, expertly trailing the dropped reins just beyond his reaching grasp.

Chapter 13

Molly Bishop, in the pleasant room that had been Laurie Jackson's, had spent an almost sleepless night. Laredo seemed not to sleep at all. A warm morning wind fanning the neat curtains at her window brought an endless murmur of sound from the saloons and the streets of the town, as men who had thronged here in these past weeks released their mounting tension and excitement. It was a constant hubbub, a tide of drunken voices and high-pitched laughter, punctuated by a smash of glass or even an occasional gunshot.

The noise wasn't what bothered her, except that it helped remind her of her failed mission, with every passing minute bringing that day's noon steadily closer. Still, she was all but resigned to that by now; it was something else that turned her thinking into a tormented muddle.

Though she tried to tell herself the Devore woman could have been lying or mistaken, in her heart she knew what she had learned about Owen Pryor must be the truth. It answered so many nagging questions—pointed up what she had been aware of as strange and less than straightforward in his behavior, and his failure to be open with her or even to suggest what he might be doing here in Laredo, even in the way he had walked away and deserted her last evening in the plaza, without so much as a word of explanation.

Almost in the act of admitting he was hardly to blame if he wanted to keep his past a secret, she found herself thinking bitterly it would be impossible to forgive his deceiving her. And an appalling thought came to her and shook her to the core: *Then am I the daughter of one outlaw, in love with another one?* She covered her face with her hands. Despite the warmth of the morning, her cheeks were cold and her hands trembled.

At last she managed to settle her thoughts on what should be her main concern—the matter of Bart Campion. She found paper and pen and, seated at the table in her nightgown, began to write—hesitantly at first and then almost feverishly as she poured out, in a letter to Bart Campion, all the unanswered questions that had perplexed her for so long. But halfway down the page her hand faltered and stopped, and at last she laid down the pen.

What was the use? Having already been refused a chance to see the man, she had no reason to believe Harry Swain would allow a message to be sent in to him. The acting sheriff would in all likelihood insist on reading it himself. That was a thought she couldn't bear, and she snatched up the unfinished letter, tore it in pieces, and dropped them into the wastebasket.

It had been a final desperate measure, and when she gave it up she felt, at last, defeated and drained.

She was still sitting there, head in hands, when a tap at the bedroom door startled her. She looked around as Sarah Jackson called hesitantly from the hallway, "Molly?

Are you awake? We're just having a bit of breakfast in the kitchen. We'd be ever so pleased if you'd join us."

She drew a breath, got her bearings. "Thank you," she answered. "I'll be glad to."

Molly dressed hurriedly. She dabbed cold water to her face, hopeful it would somehow remove the stains of a sleepless night. She ran a comb roughly through her hair and went to join her hosts.

Will Jackson was none too happy to see a day he had been dreading. "They've done their best to ruin our town," he said irritably as he speared bacon on his fork. "I hope what they're doing gets finished and over with without any hitches—then maybe we can get back to normal. I understand they got a special stagecoach set to leave an hour after the hanging for some of these people that are as anxious to leave as they were to come here in the first place. Well, they can't clear out too soon to suit me—let's have things like they used to be!"

"It will all blow over soon enough," his wife assured him. "Maybe we'll be able to forget it ever happened." Turning to Molly she said earnestly, "Just try not to pass judgment on Laredo quite yet. Wait a few days until you can see our town as it really is."

It was as good a time as any to announce the decision she had reached last night. Molly said, "I'm afraid I won't have the chance. I'm going to be leaving right away."

The old lady's coffee cup chimed against the saucer as she abruptly set it down and exclaimed, "Oh! Not so *soon?*"

"Yes," Molly said. "This afternoon, if I can get a seat on that stage."

"But, my dear! You haven't been here any time at all!"

"Long enough for me to know there's nothing in this town for me." She couldn't help a trace of bitterness creeping into her tone. "And that it would have been better if I'd never come!"

"But surely—" Sarah Jackson put out a hand to the girl, dropped it again. She appealed to her husband then. "Will! *You* speak to her!"

The old man was already studying Molly with a sober and searching glance. At what he saw in her face he shook his head regretfully. "Doesn't look like it's any use. . . ." He told Molly, "We're going to be sorry to see you go, young lady. But if your mind's made up . . ."

"I'm afraid it really is," she answered, and couldn't allow herself to look at the disappointment in Sarah Jackson's faded eyes.

Later, in her room, Molly had made her bed and set her bag on it and was stowing away the articles she had unpacked only the day before, making a careful job of it and trying to still the unhappy tumble of her thoughts. She recognized Sarah's knock at the door and opened it. The old woman saw what she was doing and said apologetically, "You're busy. I didn't mean to interrupt."

"No, no!" Molly assured her quickly. "It's perfectly all right. Did you want something?"

The old, blue-veined hands knotted together nervously. "What I *don't* want," Sarah Jackson said hesitantly, "is to seem to be talking out of turn. Will and I would hate to have you think we were interfering. But . . . do you mind if I ask, when you leave here, where will you go? Back to that rooming house you were telling me about?"

"So far as I know."

"You did say you have no people anywhere, no

138

family? Well, neither do we. Will and I, I mean. There's nobody at all left, now . . . only the two of us. We do all right, but we wonder for how much longer? We have our home here and our business, but not a soul in the world to leave them to.

"It's been very lonely," she went on, a little wistfully, while Molly wondered what point the old lady might be coming to. "Since Laurie passed away. We hardly realized *how* lonely, until now—having someone in this room, hearing a young voice in the house again! It's made *us* feel younger. I don't suppose . . ." She faltered, tried a new tack. "The thing is, we've been talking it over, and we wondered . . . We both wish you'd change your mind and stay. Make this your home, let us be your family. . . ."

Molly could only stare, unable for a moment to find any words to say. At last she managed to stammer, "Do you really mean you're suggesting I take your grand-daughter's place? Oh, I couldn't—I could never do that! Why, you don't even know me!"

"I think we do," Mrs. Jackson insisted. "Just the few hours you've been here, it seems like we've known you forever. When you go it will leave such a hole, I—I can hardly bear to think of it!" Her mouth trembled and a tear slid down a faded cheek.

Moved, Molly put out her arms and took the woman into her embrace, feeling the thinness of her body and the bones that seemed as frail as those of a bird. "Bless you!" she exclaimed. "You've been more than kind—both of you. I'll always be grateful. But if I did this, I'd just be taking advantage, and it wouldn't be fair. Though I thank you from the bottom of my heart for even suggesting it!"

They stood like that, their arms around each other, and Molly thought the old woman was weeping. But then

Sarah Jackson gave her a quick hug and stepped back. Her cheeks were wet but she was smiling brightly. "There!" she said. "You mustn't mind a sentimental old woman! You're young, you have a whole life ahead of you. No one has a right to try telling you what to do with it." On an impulse she drew Molly down to her and kissed her on the cheek.

Molly returned the kiss. "All the same," she said and meant it, "I'll never forget your offer. It's the nicest compliment anyone ever paid me!"

The morning went slowly. Somewhere in the house there was a clock that chimed the hours, and when she heard it count out eleven strokes Molly froze in what she was doing, to listen as though her heart had stopped.

She had been trying not to think any more of the man in the jail. She had tried just as hard to put out of her mind any thought of Owen Pryor, telling herself it was not likely she would be seeing him again. But when she suddenly heard Sarah Jackson calling to her, "Molly, your young man is here," she couldn't repress a quick thrill of hope. She quickly left her room and hurried to the front hallway, only to know a stab of disappointment when she saw that the person waiting beside the door was Boyce Tuthill.

She immediately felt guilty and hoped he hadn't seen what was in her face, but apparently she need not have worried. Tuthill was in the grip of some excitement, and almost before she could give a greeting he was speaking, intently and fast. "We haven't much time, and I've got to tell you what's going on."

"All right. Why don't we step out on the porch?"

"Fine!" Without ceremony he seized her arm and

140

almost dragged her outside. She could see he was flushed with the urgency of his message.

"I've just been to the jail," he said swiftly. "Talking to that fellow, Harry Swain—you know, the one that wouldn't let you see Bart Campion?" He continued without waiting for her nod. "I suppose anyone could guess why he'd be pretty much worked up right now, the closer it gets to noon! This whole thing today has been his show from the start—he arrested Campion, he strutted all through the trial, and he's turned the hanging into a public spectacle, with himself as the star.

"But now I think he's getting scared. There'll be no help from the military, and so just in case Campion's gang should actually try something, Swain's been hiring extra guards right and left—anybody who can use a gun and might be willing to help stand up to them. You'd never guess who I just saw at the courthouse, carrying a rifle and with a deputy sheriff's badge pinned to his shirt: our friend Claib Meagher!"

She stared, picturing the loudmouthed bully from the stagecoach. As he read her expression, Boyce Tuthill nodded. "You get the idea. Harry Swain is about ready to jump out of his skin just now, afraid that things can go wrong. It was all I could manage getting him quieted down enough to talk. But I did—and I've made a deal, Molly."

"Oh?" She waited, puzzled and not yet making much sense of what he was telling her.

"Concerned as he is about bringing off this hanging without any trouble, Swain is anxious as ever to get himself publicity from it if he can. Well, I've got him convinced I can do him a lot of good, according to how I write the thing up for the papers in Missouri. So, I've used a little blackmail: I've said I'll give him the story he wants, but on one condition—that he changes his mind and lets you in to see Campion!"

"You didn't!" Molly stared at him in disbelief and something like a beginning of shock. "Oh, no!"

Tuthill put a hand on her shoulder. He spoke quickly, earnestly. "I know what you're thinking, and you're wrong. I still have no idea why seeing him is so important to you—but I no longer care. Please try to believe you can trust me! I'm not after a story now. I just want to help. You mean that much to me!"

All at once she could not doubt his sincerity. "I—I do believe you," she exclaimed. "And I appreciate what you've done. But—" She shuddered. "I could never bring myself to watch—"

"You won't have to watch anything!" he assured her quickly. "It's all arranged. I'll get you inside for five minutes alone with him—I have Swain's promise. And immediately after that we can leave, before anything else happens. It's getting late, though," Tuthill added. "You're going to have to decide."

Although she hesitated, there could be but one answer. She had hoped for this too long and had come too far; she could not afford to pass it up, even though it came at the last moment and under such circumstances. Even now, she knew there was a possibility Bart Campion, himself, might refuse her the five minutes Tuthill had been able to arrange for. But the haunting question in her mind drove her on.

"It's all right," Molly said. "I've decided. . . ."

Hurried by Boyce Tuthill through the dusty streets,

142

Molly felt a knot of apprehension tightening, and her legs trembled so much that she was glad for the support of his hand grasping her arm. Every person they saw appeared to have the same destination as themselves. With each step, she became aware of a swelling of crowd noise that sounded scarcely human. And then they came out on the courthouse square and she was appalled at what confronted her.

At first glance it seemed an impenetrable mass of humanity was packed into the square. Under a blistering sun they milled about the courthouse lawn and raised a fine film of dust that hung layered above bare heads, derbies, sombreros, as well as the bonnets and parasols of a number of women who had joined the crowd. There was a hum of noisy anticipation punctuated with the brawling shouts of men who had spent the morning taking on a load of whiskey for the event.

Molly gasped and faltered. Boyce Tuthill's hold on her arm tightened and he spoke loudly, making himself heard above the noise. "We're to go right to the jail. Just leave everything to me."

He proceeded to make way for them. He did it with voice and elbow, always seeming to find a point of yielding that he could force open and propel Molly through. They were cursed and sworn at, but Tuthill had a purpose and he was unrelenting. More than once, buffeted by the press of bodies, Molly missed her footing and would have gone down except for his firm hand that held her up with a strength that surprised her.

Once she caught sight of a man with a town marshal's badge, a sweating and ineffectual-looking person who seemed to be trying to work through the mass and keep some sort of order. "Looks like Marshal Tubman is trying

143

to help out," her companion remarked, "for all the good he's doing. . . ." When they passed within a few yards of the waiting gallows Molly glimpsed its wooden framework and the steps leading up to it—there were always thirteen, she'd heard somewhere—and the crossbar with the rope that swung from it, noosed and ready. A bearded man who wore a somber black coat despite the day's heat was up there making some kind of final adjustment. She wondered if he would be the professional hangman who, she understood, had been brought to Laredo for this occasion. She shuddered and turned her eyes from him.

All at once there was an angry change in the noise of the crowd, and those in the forefront were suddenly being pushed back against Molly, alarmingly, in a way that seemed about to suffocate or trample her. She heard Boyce Tuthill's exclamation. He refused to give ground, but instead found an opening somehow and pulled her through. Then they halted, for they found themselves in the front rank and Molly could see, just ahead, the squat stone jail with its heavy wooden door.

Now, too, she could see what was happening: Men armed with guns and rifles were moving along the front of the crowd, threatening and forcing them to give ground. Despite the protests and shoving from the rear, the guards seemed to be gaining their purpose, which was to clear a way between the jail door and the foot of the gallows.

Molly stammered, "What do you suppose?—"

Tuthill's face was bleak. "I'd say Harry Swain has forgotten his promise to me! Or, maybe he's been persuaded that it isn't safe to wait till noon—he should get it over with ahead of time and have Campion safely hanged—"

Even as he spoke the hubbub around them suddenly

stilled as if it had been chopped short by a knife. The crowd fell motionless. Every eye turned toward the door of the jail.

The heavy wooden panel had opened. Men stepped out into the brilliant sunlight. There were more armed guards, a pair of them, with weapons at the ready. Behind these Molly recognized Harry Swain, the acting sheriff. She saw a man in the long, black garb of a priest, who carried a Bible and a cross. And at the center of the group, a man in shirtsleeves who walked erect with bared head defiantly lifted, despite the handcuffs glinting at his wrists.

Molly's breath caught in her throat as she stared at him. She thought he would have stood out, anywhere. He was taller than most of those around him, taller than lanky Harry Swain, and he carried himself with an uncompromising arrogance. The years had not been kind to this man. They had dug a deep furrow down either cheek and pared away the flesh until his features defined clearly the strong bone structure beneath. His hair and his mustache were grizzled, though they had been recently trimmed and he had shaved and dressed himself carefully—neither his long confinement in the Laredo jail, nor the ordeal he faced, had done anything to break Bart Campion or dim the fierceness in his deep-set eyes as he looked contemptuously over the faces turned to watch him come out and be hanged.

When one of the guards tried to hurry him forward, he gave the man a look that made him quickly drop his hand. After that, with no need of prodding, he stepped out with a firm stride. The knot of men moved into the cleared passageway, toward the gallows waiting at its end. The black-robed priest began to intone a prayer in swift-

145

flowing Latin, but Molly doubted that the prisoner gave him any attention.

And then something happened.

Campion's keen glance, mocking those who had gathered to see him die, had found Molly there at the forefront of the crowd. She caught her breath as she saw the sudden change in him. His head jerked upward, almost as though he had taken a blow. He halted in his tracks, despite the efforts of the guard to urge him on. He stood devouring her with his hard stare.

Harry Swain said irritably, "Here, now!" and took the prisoner by an elbow. Campion merely shrugged the hand away, his eyes never leaving the face of the girl before her.

He spoke then. He demanded in a harsh voice, "*Who are you?*"

Boyce Tuthill saw what was going on, and he didn't hesitate. Already he was urging Molly forward as he said loudly, "Campion, this is a girl who came a long way in hopes of seeing you—only, Harry Swain refused. This morning, at last, I thought I had his promise. But it looks as though he's broken it!"

It was unclear whether the condemned man even heard. He was looking at Molly with an intensity that appeared to close out every other sight or sound. Harry Swain was glaring angrily at Tuthill's interruption, and now one of the guards came striding over.

It was Claib Meagher; it gave him obvious satisfaction to place a big hand against Boyce Tuthill's chest and shove him roughly aside. "Get back!" he ordered loudly. "Unless you want me to flatten you again. We're taking nothing off you—or her highness, either. D'you—"

The words died on his lips. He stumbled, and his

head jerked backward. His knees buckled. He twisted as he fell, and as she saw the blood on his chest Molly Bishop's choked scream mingled with the echoes of the rifle shot that killed him.

Chapter 14

Owen Pryor had no clear idea of the time, except that he was sure it must be closing in on noon. But when he rode into Laredo's outskirts, pushing hard, he saw no undue amount of excitement and this gave him hope that it wasn't yet too late. He had been pleased, if surprised, to find his own chestnut gelding left tethered in the brush beside the stage road. Across his knees he carried the rifle from the saddle scabbard on Merl Loomis's roan.

Instead of heading directly for the jail, he took a moment to go to the house where Molly Bishop was staying. Whatever else might happen, he had to satisfy himself that she would be all right. As Pryor rode up, Mrs. Jackson had just stepped out upon the porch to shake a dustrag. He reined in and touched his hat brim. "Ma'am," he said, "if Miss Bishop will see me, I'd admire to have a word with her."

The old lady frowned at him. "But, she's not here. I saw her leave a few minutes ago, with another gentleman—that Mr. Tuthill."

"Where?"

She hesitated. "I'm not certain, but I have an idea they were headed for the courthouse. And I'm really a little worried. I don't think it's any place for her—not at a time like—"

Mrs. Jackson did not finish, for Pryor had kicked his horse and was gone before she could get it out.

In his concern for Jim Dance, it had never once occurred to him that Molly, too, might be in any peril. Bart Campion's hanging was certainly the last thing she would have wanted to see. All he could think was that this must be Boyce Tuthill's doing! If that news-hungry reporter had led her into danger, Pryor would have it out of his hide.

He sent the chestnut pounding through nearly deserted streets. The distance was only a couple of blocks, yet it seemed endless. He came in on the northeast corner of the square, which put the big courthouse on his left and gave him an instant view of what was happening at the jail. He pulled in his mount so sharply that the horse tossed its head in protest.

"Damn!" he spat out.

Harry Swain was jumping the gun, going ahead with the hanging, not waiting for noon! The first person Pryor recognized was Bart Campion, standing spare and erect, head and shoulders above the armed men accompanying him to the gallows. He glimpsed the photographer, set up and fussing with his equipment, getting ready for a shot. He anxiously looked for Molly but couldn't find her; she would be engulfed in the press of men surrounding her. But there was Tuthill! That meant she had to be here! Pryor was about to kick his horse and drive straight into the mob blocking his way, in search of her, when he heard the first shot.

It came from somewhere above and to his right. He saw the man who took the bullet—it was one of the armed guards and looked almost like big Claib Meagher. Pryor didn't wait to watch him fall.

When he tried to turn his horse the confused animal

went clear around in a circle before he could get it settled. He brought up the saddle gun. He had spotted a film of smoke and next moment he located the sniper squatting on a rooftop just at the corner of a building's tall false front. The thought occurred to him: *That could be Jim Dance!* He closed his mind to it. With the weapon at his shoulder he snapped off a shot, worked the lever, and fired again. The dark shape on the roof fell back and vanished. The man up there had lost his rifle, and it came sliding down across the shingles, sunlight bouncing from the barrel as it spun.

The chestnut didn't much like gunfire, and the crowd was roaring and screaming, breaking for cover. The horse tried to act up and again Pryor had to settle it. At the same time he spotted a second figure atop a neighboring building; he fired hastily, came close enough to make that one duck wildly out of sight. He was just levering a fresh shell into the chamber when suddenly he realized the other marksmen stationed by Duke Ridge around these two adjoining sides of the square had gone to work. Rifles cracked in rapid succession.

That opening shot had been only the starting signal. Pryor hurriedly searched along the low rooftops and picked out a few bursts of powder smoke, but scattering echoes made it hard to judge how many snipers there were. Meanwhile, down in the square, everything was pandemonium.

In front of the jail the sound of men yelling interspersed with the screams of women, as the crowd tried to scatter in a single trampling rush. Pryor glimpsed the photographer scurrying for cover, lugging his bulky camera and a box of glass plates. Some, like barnyard fowl under the shadow of a chicken hawk, stood befuddled, not knowing which way to run, and one of these was

Harry Swain. The acting sheriff appeared rooted to the ground, a man in shock who didn't seem to hear his men shouting at him and begging for orders. Seeing that, Pryor swore and started for him.

Bullets were kicking up spatters of dust, but a few crumpled shapes lying motionless or writhing on the ground already showed that some of the snipers were hunting actual targets. Even now another of the men guarding the prisoner spun and dropped. Swain didn't seem to notice. He merely stared, uncomprehending, at the horseman bearing down on him.

"Damn you!" Owen Pryor shouted above the confusion. "Wake up! Get these men under cover! Campion's gang is going to hit you and take your prisoner!"

The acting sheriff gave no sign he even heard. But just beyond, standing with the glint of the handcuffs on his wrists, Bart Campion was listening, and when his glance crossed Pryor's it held recognition. Beyond any shadow of doubt he remembered the Salado Kid. Whether or not he'd had any hint of a plan to rescue him, he couldn't help but realize that Owen Pryor was trying to prevent it. That knowledge was in the look that flashed between them.

Then Harry Swain broke free of shock. All at once he was yelling commands: "Get Campion back inside and prepare to fort up. By God, we'll be ready for them!" There was no need for urging. In a burst of activity the prisoner was jerked about and hustled toward the jail entrance. Pryor turned to look for Molly Bishop.

At least she wasn't among the casualties. One of these, he saw now, actually was Claib Meagher. The black-robed priest kneeling beside him, oblivious to his own peril, told Pryor the big man must be dead. He continued his anxious search. Just then someone ran in front of his horse, and the frightened animal squealed and tried to rear and had to be hauled down again.

Moments later he found what he had been desperately hunting for.

Molly and Boyce Tuthill had taken shelter beneath the platform of the deserted gallows. The sight of her crouching there filled him with something close to fury—and now a shot fired from the roof of a harness shop just opposite looked, from his angle, to have been aimed directly at her. He brought up his own weapon, but when he triggered nothing happened. The rifle was shot dry; he flung it aside and yanked out his belt gun, though the range was much too far for a pistol.

The man on the harness shop fired again, and this time he actually saw a yellow splinter of wood go flying from one of the timbers near Molly's head. At that all his controls snapped, and Pryor rammed home the spur.

With men scattering wildly out of his path, he rounded the scaffold and leaped his horse into the street, pointing straight for the harness shop. The sniper saw him coming and immediately switched his target, but Pryor held off until he was in sure range. The man shot at him—too hastily and too high. Hauling rein with his chestnut's front hoofs almost on the wooden sidewalk, Pryor flung his gun-arm straight up and fired twice. The second bullet found its mark. The rifle popped out of the sniper's hands as he was flung backward onto the slant of the roof. From there he came rolling limply down, struck a wooden awning, and dropped to the ruts of the street. Lying face down, he had something about him that looked very much like Jim Dance.

Pryor had to know. The breath was shallow in his chest as he curbed the frightened horse and leaped down. Keeping hold of the reins he got to the man he had shot and turned the body over. As he did the head rolled loosely, making him fight a brief rise of sickness. But the man wasn't Jim Dance. It was no one he had ever seen before, and Pryor was able to breathe again.

Scarcely a full minute had elapsed since the shooting began spreading panic and confusion through the courthouse square. Now it ceased, as abruptly as it started, and Pryor knew what that meant. A swelling of pounding hooves announced the second part of Duke Ridge's rescue operation. At a gallop, horsemen came spilling through the gap between a pair of buildings. Pryor counted seven, with the stocky shape of Duke Ridge in the lead and an extra mount, under saddle, for carrying Bart Campion to freedom.

They came sweeping in, in the grand manner, with a spattering of pistol shots and a Rebel yell that would have done credit to a Confederate cavalry charge. It had been well planned; given the element of surprise, it could have worked, would have, probably, except for Owen Pryor's warning. Now, watching from beneath the awning of the harness shop, he knew who was going to be surprised.

Campion's men had reached the open space before the jail, and there they pulled in. He could imagine their perplexity, finding it deserted and no one in sight. They milled about, trying to hold their nervous animals while dust swirled and thinned around them in the noonday heat. Pryor spotted Jim Dance. There was a mere glimpse of him on his black horse before someone else came between. Pryor slowly lowered his gun. There was no way he could bring himself to fire into that clot of men and horses, not with Jim Dance a part of it.

Someone in the jail, though, had no such compunctions. A pistol flashed fire from one of the barred windows, and a rider was knocked backward over the cantle of his saddle and hit the ground spread-eagled. At once a barrage opened up, and at that the riders broke apart like a billiard setup split by the cue ball. Even so they tried to return the fire. Duke Ridge was yelling, attempting to rally them; a few did respond and actually started an effort to rush the building. But in the open, against men barricaded behind heavy stone, they had no chance at all. In the end they could only retreat, and they began to do so, still shooting as they fell back.

By this time, horses whose owners had left them at hitching racks around the square were squealing frantically and fighting their tethers. One had broken loose and it came galloping toward Pryor with reins and stirrups flopping, briefly obstructing his view. He ran out into the street for a better vantage point.

Now that those in the jail seemed to have the outlaws in trouble, at least some of the crowd that had scattered into hiding must be getting their nerve back. They had laid hold of weapons, and suddenly Campion's men were finding themselves harassed by gunfire from windows and doorways. It built to a tremendous crescendo. Bart Campion's men knew they were in a hopeless situation. They milled indecisively. When a horse took a bullet and went plowing into the dirt with its rider, that settled the matter. With one accord the outlaws turned to make a getaway.

The rider of the fallen horse rolled to his feet and he went running after them. Someone found courage enough to turn back, reach down, and haul the man up behind him. The horse with its double burden joined the ragged scatter as the Campion gang spurred all-out past the courthouse, took the corner at Farragut, and went streaming south along Convent Avenue at a wild gallop. The river lay that way.

The attempt to rescue their chief had ended in fiasco. But their dust settled on a courthouse square that had all the appearance of a battlefield.

Doors slammed and already men were pouring into the street, carrying guns and yelling in high-pitched excitement. Owen Pryor caught up the reins of his horse and led it across to where Tuthill and Molly stood in the shadow of the gallows. Her head was down and the reporter's hands lay on her shoulders; he seemed to be trying to comfort her. Pryor said anxiously, "Molly! Are you all right?"

She looked around and saw him. Her eyes were enormous in a face gone white with fear. At once she turned away from Boyce Tuthill and reached out to Pryor as she exclaimed, " *You* weren't hurt?"

"Of course not."

"I was so afraid. . . ."

Tuthill said, "We saw you start after that man on the roof, and she couldn't bear to watch."

Pryor turned to his horse then, mounted quickly. The square gradually was filling again, far more slowly than it had emptied. "Get her clear of this!" he told Tuthill. He picked an impatient route through the men straggling out from cover, and then he had put the courthouse behind him and was riding in the wake of the vanished outlaws.

Chapter 15

Pryor didn't actually have it in mind to catch up with them. They had too much of a lead. Besides he was sure all they wanted, after their defeat and utter rout at the jail, was to get out of this town and put the river and the Mexican border behind them.

He took the half-dozen blocks at his own pace. He rode by the plaza that lay empty now with its bandstand deserted and the scaffolding around the old cathedral rising into the hot noontime sky. And so he came out upon the bluff above the Rio Grande, where he reined in.

The ferry was tied at the opposite bank, and the outlaws hadn't waited for it. They'd put their horses into the river and were making strong headway against its sluggish current. Pryor watched them go, noting that their numbers had grown—that meant at least some of the snipers had escaped from the roofs and joined them. The high sun's glare made a smear of brown water that turned the horses and their riders into mere black shapes, impossible to recognize. Held up as they were by their swimming horses, he supposed with a rifle he might have been able to pick off some of them, but a handgun was useless at the distance, and in any event, he wouldn't have tried.

There had been enough killing for one day. And

there was no way he could have been sure which of those fugitives down there was Jim Dance.

Sitting with the damp breath of the river rising to him in the muggy stillness, he felt the tension of these past hours begin to slip from him. He drew off his hat and ran a sleeve across his sweating forehead. Then, hearing some-one riding up to the edge of the bluff beside him, he quickly turned. He stiffened slightly as he saw that the man in the saddle of the other horse, a rangy claybank, was Bill Longley.

Pryor pulled his hat on and let his hand drop near the butt of his holstered gun. He studied the face of the other man—the piercing eyes and sardonic set of the mouth—as Longley drew rein and looked at the horses and riders approaching the farther bank.

The gunman said dryly, "So! That's the end of Bart Campion's gang."

"Are you sure? Looks to me there's quite a number of them left."

Longley shrugged. "Without Bart, the rest are nothing—less than nothing! After this fiasco Duke Ridge will never get anybody to follow him. And no one else is strong enough, or smart enough, to take over instead—including your friend Jim Dance." He shook his head. "No, I'll give you even money that come nightfall, that outfit will have split and scattered for good."

Pryor gave the man a look. "Were you at the courthouse just now? I never saw you."

"I didn't mean to be seen. But, oh yes—I was there. From what I saw, the scheme to set Campion loose might have worked if you hadn't been on hand." Pryor didn't try to judge whether that was meant as a compliment or condemnation. He made no answer, and Longley said, "Well, I guess Harry Swain will have another try at taking

Bart Campion out and hanging him. This time he should manage."

Pryor drew a breath. He said reluctantly, "I suppose I'd better get back." But before turning away he had a final look at the river, where the first of the fleeing outlaws were already climbing out upon the opposite bank—safe now from pursuit by Texas law.

When he picked up the reins, he saw that Bill Longley made no move to join him. "You're not coming?"

The gunman shook his head. "I prefer not to watch hangings. Someday, one of them might be my own!" He looked curiously at Pryor. "You suppose we'll be meeting again?"

"Not likely. The Salado Kid is as dead as any of the rest of the gang."

Longley thought that over. Then, without expression, he gave a twitch of the bridles that sent his horse toward the dug road that led off the bluff and down to the level of the river. Pryor watched him only for a moment. With other pressures on him, he spoke to his mount and reined away in the direction of the courthouse square.

He found things there in confusion, with Marshal Tubman hurrying about trying to keep order. By now most of the crowd had reassembled, aware that the spectacle they were here for had only been postponed, but while they waited they had plenty to occupy them. A few stood and stared silently at a couple of bodies that someone had had consideration enough to cover with blankets; others gathered about the carcass of the dead horse and debated the best way of getting the thing hauled off and disposed of. But the largest group had collected where the itinerant photographer had set up his tripod and camera, and on noticing Boyce Tuthill there, Owen Pryor tied his horse and walked over.

He saw then what occupied the center of attention. Three dead outlaws had been laid side-by-side, bloodied by the bullet wounds that had finished them, their heads propped up so the camera could get their faces into the picture. To Pryor it was a barbaric procedure, but one he knew was customary on this Western frontier. Tuthill stopped beside him and said briefly, "Well there's the tally—three of Campion's gang dead. The one on the left, I saw you kill. The middle one got shot off his horse when they charged the jail. The third was found dead in the alley. Another of the snipers, apparently—it looks as though you did in that one, too. All the rest got away."

Pryor made no comment; he was feeling a little sickened at the thought that he had actually killed three men today, beginning with Merl Loomis. Two of these men here were total strangers to him. The raider who had been knocked off in the first volley from the jail had been Duke Ridge's tracker, Esteban. All of them were new since his time with the gang—it showed how drastically the personnel of such an outfit could change in a few short years.

He had seen enough, and he turned away. He asked Tuthill, "Where's Molly?"

For answer, the other man pointed to where a doctor had his black bag open and was working on someone who had taken a bullet in the random gunfire. The hurt man's shirt had been cut away and a bandage was being put in place on his shoulder and upper arm. And there was Molly Bishop, with the sleeves of her blouse rolled up, on her knees beside the doctor and helping him in his work.

Tuthill said, "I tried to get her to leave, but she wouldn't, not when she saw something she could do. She's really game, Pryor, as game and brave as they come."

Pryor's face was stiff with anger. "It still doesn't

excuse you bringing her here today! If anything had happened—"

"I can explain, if you give me a chance," the newspaperman said coldly. "Are you willing to listen?"

"All right."

"For some reason no one has bothered explaining to *me,* Molly Bishop had her mind set on seeing Bart Campion. Much as I disapprove, I had developed some leverage with Swain, and I used it to make him agree to let her have what she wanted. That's why I brought her to the jail. But then, at the last minute Swain apparently changed his mind. We were waiting for him to keep his promise when he came out with Campion and the priest, heading for the gallows. And, d'you know, it was the damnedest thing—"

"What?"

"Bart Campion took one look at Molly and it was almost as though he had seen a ghost! He stopped in his tracks and I heard him saying, 'Who are you?' Now, what would you make of that?"

Owen Pryor, staring, found himself remembering Molly's words to him: *I've always looked just like my mother. . . .* "What else did he say?" he demanded.

"Nothing—that's when the shooting started. Since then, with so much going on, I haven't had a chance to get at Harry Swain again to remind him of his promise."

"Where is he now?"

"Over at the jail, I guess."

Pryor said, "I think maybe I'll have a word with him."

Boyce Tuthill gave him a look and a shrug. "Go ahead. Molly would rather you helped her than me," he admitted in a heavy tone. "She's been making it pretty clear which of us two she prefers. I don't have to like it, you understand; but that's how it is." He hesitated before reluctantly adding, "And, who knows—perhaps she's right. Perhaps she'd be better suited to someone more like you."

Pryor took a moment to consider this other man. They were likely too far apart in background and in ambition ever really to be friends, even if there had been no unspoken rivalry caused by the presence of Molly Bishop. But he meant it when he said slowly, "You're a good man, Tuthill."

Their eyes met. The newspaperman only nodded and turned about his business. Pryor headed for the jail.

The door opened as he approached and Harry Swain emerged. A man came hurrying just then, carrying a rifle, and the two of them were examining it when Pryor walked up. He recognized it instantly, of course, by the letters worked out on the butt in brass-headed tacks: "M. L." It was the weapon he himself had used against the snipers on the roofs around the square and had flung aside when it was empty.

When Swain looked up and saw Pryor he instantly stiffened. Pryor, without preliminary, pointed to the rifle and said, "I can tell you about that. I took it off one of Bart Campion's men—a fellow named Loomis. You can see the initials."

Swain reacted to the name. "Merl Loomis? Hell, I know who *he* is!"

"Was," Owen Pryor corrected him.

"He's dead?"

"This morning—he made a try for me, but I was lucky. There's an abandoned ranch about an hour's ride north of here," Pryor went on. "You can find him there, if you want him—I put his body in the house, to keep the varmints off."

Harry Swain was scowling fiercely, while his man stood by gawking from one speaker to the other. The acting sheriff had had a tough morning, and he looked a shade bewildered by all of it. He rubbed a fist along his lantern jaw and said harshly, "And so you've turned against your own kind!"

Pryor's mouth hardened. He said coldly, "Put it any way you like, Harry. Fact remains, I learned the plan for taking Bart Campion, otherwise you'd have lost him."

"That's a lie!"

But the bluster failed a little under Pryor's steady regard. He continued: "I think we both know the truth. You owe me a debt and I'm calling it in—right now. There's a girl who has been trying to get a word with Campion. I understand you finally agreed but then backed out. I'm asking you to go ahead and keep your promise."

Harry Swain's jaw thrust forward but there was no real argument in him. "I don't like it," he said petulantly. "I don't like any part of something I don't understand. All the same, Campion caught a glimpse of that girl and now as a last favor he's asked me to let them have five minutes if I can find her. So it looks like—" He shrugged. "Oh, hell! You know where she's at?"

"I'll fetch her," Pryor said.

The doctor had completed his work on the injured man and was packing his bag. Pryor took Molly by the arm and helped her to rise, and as she brushed off her skirt he said, "Come with me."

He didn't explain; walking beside him, she looked at him in puzzlement. But as they neared the jail and she saw Harry Swain scowling in the doorway, she must have guessed what was up. Suddenly he was aware she had begun to tremble.

162

Harry Swain told her gruffly, "All right! You get what you wanted. But, make it quick—we've lost enough time!"

She tried to thank him but could only nod. She was suddenly pale, and with some reluctance Pryor suggested, "Do you want me to come in with you?"

Molly grasped at the offer. "I wouldn't have suggested it, but, would you?"

"Of course." It had never occurred to him that he would have to meet Bart Campion again face-to-face, but to give this girl reassurance he would go to almost any limit.

Harry Swain, however, continued to block their way. He pointed to the gun in Pryor's holster. "Not till you give me that!"

Reluctantly, Pryor drew the gun and handed it over, butt first.

The lawman shoved the gun behind his waistband and gestured them into the building ahead of him.

Pryor knew these stone walls were just as solid as they looked; the two narrow cells were like steel cages, one empty now but the other's shadowy interior giving a glimpse of its lone occupant. "You can do your talking through the bars," Swain said. "You've got exactly five minutes—then I'll be back." He was pulling out a silver watch as he backed through the doorway with a lingering and suspicious glance. Obviously he trusted none of this. For their part, Pryor and the girl forgot him immediately.

A man moved into the light from the shadows at the rear of one of the cells and took hold of the bars. At closer hand, now, it was easier to see the changes in him. Bart Campion looked thinner, older than a few years should have made him. Pryor was reminded of the crime that had put him here, and of the way Ed Donnelly's widow had described him at his trial: *I'm not at all sure that the man I saw sitting in that courtroom like a caged wolf was entirely sane!*

But if there was a glint of madness in his eyes, it was clear enough that Campion not only knew the man he faced but also the part Owen Pryor had played in thwarting his one chance of rescue and of escaping the gallows. That knowledge was in the glittering stare the outlaw gave him. Then, without saying anything, Bart Campion turned his attention to the girl. She looked back at him as though unable to speak now that the moment she had waited for was actually here.

Pryor gave her elbow a gentle squeeze to encourage her. "Go ahead. . . ."

Molly drew a breath. She began in a tone that showed the strain she was under. "Mister Campion, when you looked at me a while ago I thought I reminded you of someone. I'm wondering if it could have been someone a good time back—before the war. Perhaps a girl you knew once, over around Nacogdoches County. A girl named Lorena . . ."

Bart Campion's breathing sounded harsh in the dead stillness of the jail. At last he spoke, to exclaim roughly, "How do you come to know so much about me?"

"Man, haven't you guessed even yet?" Pryor said. "This is Molly Bishop—Lorena's daughter!"

The man in the cell flicked him the briefest glance, as though annoyed. It was a moment before anyone said anything more. Then Campion asked the girl in a slightly altered tone, "How is your mother?"

"She died two years ago."

"Oh . . ." And when he'd absorbed that: "And how about old Tom?"

"You knew him, too?" the girl quickly exclaimed and got his brief nod. "My fa—Tom Bishop went off to the war when I was barely old enough to remember him. He was killed fighting in the wilderness. Mother and I have been alone ever since. And now, there's just me."

Her voice faltered. Bart Campion continued to study her intently but he asked no further questions and offered no comment. Hearing the sounds that drifted into this stillness where noontime heat pressed upon them from the low ceiling overhead, Owen Pryor felt he had to move the moment along, difficult as he knew it must be for the girl. He reminded her quietly, "There isn't too much time, Molly. I think you better ask the question you came for."

She nodded. She had to make a couple of attempts to get the words spoken. "Mister Campion, the thing I'm trying to say is that, even though I carry his name, Tom Bishop has never seemed very real to me. I have hardly any memories of him . . . he seems some kind of stranger. But on the other hand, what I heard about *you* through the years, from my mother—"

"She talked about me?"

"Oh, yes! Though often it wasn't so much what she said as . . . the things she *didn't* say. Like—" Molly hesitated, then blurted it out. "Like the times when she didn't know I was watching, and I'd see her looking at a headline in the paper about something you had done— and she'd be crying!"

Observing him closely, Pryor saw the change that came over the man's face, seeming to deepen the lines carved there. The knuckles of the fingers clutching the steel bars whitened with his grip. And then, on an impulse, Molly placed her hand on one of his as she said urgently, "Believe me, I would never have come to you

165

with this, but now you're my only hope of knowing what I was never able to ask her while she lived. Please—tell me the truth! *Could* I be your daughter?"

For a moment there was no reaction, but then it came and it was nearly violent. "*No!*" Bart Campion jerked his hands away from the door and from her touch. He said it again: "*No!* Why would you want to think you were any part of *me?* Sure, I knew Lorena Wakeman. Maybe I was in love with her, once. But I was nothing—a wild young hellion, headed no-place, and . . . and not near good enough . . . for her! Then another man came along, a hell of a lot better man in every way. Girl, you ought to be proud to carry Tom Bishop's name! The world would of been better off if he'd lived instead of me. I can say that, because I knew him—and, would I lie to build up the man who took Lorena Wakeman from me?"

"Then, Tom Bishop really *was* my father?"

"Ain't that what I been trying to tell you?"

He glared at her with a look that seemed almost to hold a mad fury. She hardly appeared to notice. Pryor could see a dramatic transformation taking place before his eyes. He had known the deep uncertainties that drove this girl; now Bart Campion had given her an answer that satisfied her needs and was already starting its work in the faint flush that colored her cheek. "How can I thank you?" she cried. "You can't possibly know what you've done, just setting my mind at rest at last!"

That was when Swain's coarse voice came to them from beyond the jail doorway. "You, in there! Your time's about up!" Molly's eyes widened. A gasp of dismay broke from her, as though she suddenly remembered where she was and what awaited this man in the cell.

Quickly, Pryor took her shoulders and turned her away, calling an answer as he did so: "She's coming!" To

Molly he said quietly, "We have to leave. But wait for me outside. I'd like a last word with him." She nodded blindly; he saw a shine of tears before she turned her head and let him guide her to the door.

He looked again at Campion and saw the outlaw had his face pressed to the bars to get a last glimpse of the girl. "Bart," Pryor said and brought the mad and sunken eyes to him. For a moment these two men—the murderer and the man who had prevented his break for freedom— looked at each other with complete understanding. Pryor said: "I'll look after her."

"Do that, Kid," the outlaw said. And then he added, swiftly and fiercely, "I never could have!"

There was nothing more for either man to say.

Chapter 16

Pryor's next urgency was to get the girl away from that place as soon as possible. Already a new head of expectancy and excitement was growing. By now the dead and wounded from the aborted raid had been removed, and the crowd filling the square sensed that there couldn't be much more reason for delay.

He kept a close eye on Molly as they walked the few blocks from the courthouse, he leading the chestnut, the girl with head lowered, silent in the grip of her feelings. For himself, Pryor was aware of the passing of these moments that might be the last they would ever have. He rehearsed a dozen things to say but discarded them all.

When finally they reached the little house where the Jacksons lived, she halted and turned to him, and seeing the pallor in her cheeks he was moved to say, "You sure you're all right?" She nodded, with the most fleeting of smiles. He persisted. "What will you do now?"

She roused herself to answer: "Take the very first stage out of here. Try to forget I ever saw this town!"

"There are a couple of things I've been wanting to say. Will you let me have a few minutes?"

"Of course," Molly agreed, with a look of surprise. Pryor left his horse on grounded reins, and they went up the path to the bench before the house. They sat there a moment without speaking. Molly was still preoccupied and he knew very well what it was that troubled her. All at once there was a sound—not really a shout, more like a murmur of trapped breath issuing from a hundred throats, and loud enough to carry across the town. Molly's head jerked up. With a gasp, she flung herself upon Pryor's breast, and he slipped an arm awkwardly about her shoulders as he felt sobs shake her.

"It's over now," he said soothingly. "It's all over."

Recovering, Molly drew away as though embarrassed at her own behavior. She took a handkerchief from a pocket of her shirtwaist and used it to dry her eyes and mop her cheeks. She blew her nose, and a last shuddering spasm went through her. "I know," she said in a dull tone. "And it had to be done. But . . . I can't help the way I feel, knowing that only a few minutes ago I was *talking* to him. And he did give me back my father!"

Pryor looked at her quickly. Yes, it was clear that she believed Campion. She had taken what the man had given her at face value, not guessing the real meaning of the sacrifice he had made. And that was just as well.

He drew a breath and set himself for what he had to do. "Molly, I told you there was something I wanted to say—something I've been holding back. Not that I actually lied to you, I'd never do that. But I have left a lot unsaid and I don't feel right about it." He went on swiftly, to have it out. "The fact is, I once knew Bart Campion. I was even a member of his gang, and I served two years in prison for bank robbery. There—now it's said!" And he forced himself to meet her eyes.

He couldn't fathom the look she gave him. He saw no trace of shock nor of disbelief. Instead, a hint of a smile trembled on her lips and she said solemnly, "Why—thank you, Owen. I had decided you were never going to tell me. I was trying not to let it make a difference."

Pryor could only stare. "You *knew?*"

"Since last evening. I heard it, sitting on this very bench, from a woman who called herself Cherry Devore. . . ."

He repeated the name, stunned.

"She'd seen the two of us and recognized you—she even told me a name the members of the gang used to know you by. She asked me what you and I were doing in Laredo—she'd heard I was trying to see Bart Campion and wanted to know why. I told her."

Pryor shook his head, struggling with his feelings. Cherry Devore! He hadn't once thought of her in all of this; he would probably have said she was either dead by now or had drifted on somewhere as such women did, completely out of touch with the members of the gang.

Beside him, the girl was waiting silently; he could almost feel her troubled regard. He got abruptly to his feet, moved a restless pace away, and stopped with his back to her.

"Why I came to Laredo," he told her gruffly, "is a long story that doesn't matter much now. What does matter is that Cherry Devore told you the truth. And as it happened I ran into the leaders of the gang here, and I learned how they meant to free Campion. I decided I had to try and stop them. Maybe, some day," he added heavily, "I'll be able to quit feeling like a traitor—"

"But those people they shot down!" Molly said in a voice that sounded stifled by remembered horror. "Even a bully like Claib Meagher deserved better than that!" She added, "Besides, I can't believe you would do anything

that you weren't sure was right. If you've made mistakes I
know you learned from them."

"I'd like to think so. It's hard to know sometimes.
Like my reason for coming here to Laredo: *That* was a
mistake, all the way around. Or it would have been,
except for one thing . . ."

"What do you mean?"

He came around then to face her. "It has to do with
the other thing I wanted to talk to you about. If you have
time to listen."

"Why, Owen! What a thing to say! You know I'd
always *make* time!"

"Well . . ." He plunged ahead. "I've told you about
my place in New Mexico. I'm working hard, trying to
make up, I guess, for the wrong start I took. So far it don't
amount to a lot; but I intend that it will! I've got grass and
water, proved up on or under lease. The calf drop this
spring was the best yet. A house I built is comfortable
enough, with shade trees started. Two rooms so far, and
I'll be adding more. I've even got a spring piped into the
kitchen.

"It's all sort of primitive yet, and it needs a woman's
touch, and . . . I thought you . . ."

Pryor broke off as he saw the girl's frown. "I don't
think I understand you," Molly said, hesitant. "Are you
. . . offering me a job as your housekeeper?"

Pryor felt his face starting to grow warm. "Good
Lord, no!" he exclaimed. "You don't understand at all!
It's my fault. I've never had any experience at proposing
marriage."

That brought her off the bench, to come and peer
closely into his face. "You want to marry *me?*"

"Maybe I haven't the right on such short notice. But

171

that's how it is," he said stubbornly. "If we were back East someplace, I might have been able to go about it right—bring you flowers and sit in the parlor, and after a while maybe hire a buggy and team to take you out for rides. Out here, though, things can't always be that cut and dried.

"Why, a neighbor of mine in New Mexico married a woman he'd never even seen! All there'd been between them was a few letters back and forth. Just the same, he had the preacher ready when the stage rolled in. In an hour they were man and wife and on their way out to his ranch. That was last year—and so far, the marriage has worked out fine."

He went on, beginning to smile, "But just look at the advantage I've got on him! I've known you almost two whole days—"

She was studying him carefully, her eyes bright and a becoming flush heightening the color of her cheeks. And as his smile faded, she said gently, "I've liked you, Owen, from the first talk we had, there in the dusk at the stage station."

"Then? . . ." With her face so near his own, it seemed the natural thing—like the sealing of a bargain—that he should bend his head and kiss her. It was a tentative kiss but her lips were soft and warm. Afterward, without touching her or taking her in his arms, he drew back and Molly smiled at him.

Pryor said roughly, "Look! I don't want to rush you into something before you're really sure. Maybe you should make up your mind after you've seen the house."

"But I'm not marrying a house," she told him. "I'm marrying a man. And—I'm sure!"

"I know *I* am!" But now, regretfully, practicalities bore in on them and brought them back to earth. Pryor checked the time by the hang of the sun. He said, "I guess we've got some planning to do! Tell me—is it absolutely necessary that you go back to that boardinghouse?"

She considered. "No, I don't suppose so. I haven't any belongings there that couldn't be sent on to me."

"Good! Because then there's no real need of bucking the mob that's sure to be on that stage this afternoon."

"I wasn't looking forward to it!" Molly admitted. She hesitated. "Would you like to know what just occurred to me?"

"Go ahead."

"I'm thinking, if you have no objection, I'd sort of like for us to be married here—in Laredo. And I'd like to ask Mr. and Mrs. Jackson if they'll stand up with us."

This time it was a common impulse that drew them together. They stayed in each other's arms for a long moment, and after the kiss Molly drew back flushed and with eyes shining. Pryor caught both her hands and held them for an instant as he told her soberly, "I think I'm only beginning to realize just what a lucky fellow I am!"

Promising to hurry back, Pryor set off to arrange the wedding. Riding away from there, he was surprised at the little time that had actually elapsed since their talk with Bart Campion in the jail. These dusty streets were alive, just now, with spectators straggling away from the courthouse square. Some were voluble with comment, as though what they had just witnessed had been a show put on for their benefit; others seemed silent and subdued. After all, they had witnessed more of death this day than any of them had reckoned on, and it was a thing many of these men would not soon get over.

Thinking of one person who, in all likelihood, had been forgotten in the day's events, on an impulse Pryor went a little out of his way and approached the house with the white picket fence that stood alone near the timbered bank of Zacate Creek. Kate Donnelly must have seen him from the window, and as he dismounted she came hurrying out to him. Holding the chestnut's reins, he said, "I only dropped by for a moment. I thought you might not have had any word."

"Is it over?" she demanded, studying his face.

"All over."

Sheriff Donnelly's widow lifted her gaunt shoulders with a sigh. She shook her head. "I suppose I could feel vengeful about it," she commented slowly, "but if I feel anything at all, it's not that! More sad than anything else, I suppose. Bart Campion could have had good things in him—Ed always claimed so. When you think about it, they were both among the last casualties of that damned war!"

"And not the only ones," Pryor said. "I guess you didn't hear what happened just before Bart was hanged."

"I heard some shooting. Did it mean what I was afraid it did?"

He nodded and told her the gang made their try.

They talked a little longer, and Kate Donnelly congratulated him on his plans for marriage. As he prepared to leave, she watched him turn away to mount, then said quickly: "Tell me, do you by any chance expect to be seeing Harry Swain? I have a message—I just now saw a stray horse that came dragging his reins along the creek bank, not more than ten minutes ago. He was all lathered up and didn't much want to get caught, but there wasn't anybody else around to do it so I ran out and caught him. I wonder if he might have got away from one of Campion's men."

Pryor almost smiled—he had a sharp mental picture

174

of this determined, rawboned woman exerting her will and main strength to bring a frightened bronc under control. "Where have you got him?"

"Tied to that big sycamore, around the side of the house. You want a look?"

As he followed her around the house she was saying, "He's a good horse. A big fellow—black as coal. Has one of those Mexican saddles. I don't think I ever saw so much silver trimming. . . ." But Owen Pryor scarcely heard. For now he saw the black, standing droop-headed with the sweat gleaming on his sides and the sunlight, filtered by tree branches, picking glints of light from the charro saddle's massive silver pommel.

And he knew at once Jim Dance had never made it across the river.

There was little traffic along the creek bank and at first the tracks weren't hard to follow. The terrified black had left an erratic trail up from the south, leading him toward the river; but all too soon it merged with the powdery dust of one of Laredo's streets, and here he lost the sign completely. Pryor drew in, baffled, and still with no hint as to what might have happened to Jim Dance. Even after losing his horse, he could have managed to catch up and ride double with one of the other outlaws. Maybe he was away and safe after all.

It was a blind hunch more than any clue supplied by the black's course of flight that made Pryor think of one place he might look. He rode another block, into the Mexican quarter. When Conchita's adobe shack came into sight, standing apart from its nearest neighbors, it looked deserted. So he was sure that he had drawn a blank, but he rode on up meaning to call out and learn if the girl might be inside. And then the words died in his throat.

The weeds grew rank and high and he was almost on top of the body before he caught sight of it, crumpled and motionless within a yard of the closed front door. Instantly he was down from the saddle. Jim Dance lay with eyes closed in a face like parchment. When Pryor saw the bloody damage from the bullet that had struck him in the chest, he was sure at first his friend was dead; then he caught the faint movement of breathing, and the hurt man opened his eyes.

He peered up at Pryor for a moment, without recognition. "Hey, cowboy!" he said hoarsely. Suddenly a look of alarm crossed his sweaty features and he managed to lift a hand shakily. "Don't walk away, cowboy!" he pleaded. "Don't leave me!"

Pryor went down on one knee. "Don't you know me, Jim?"

The wandering stare seemed to bring Pryor into focus. "It's the Kid!" he exclaimed. "But, how'd you get *here?* I thought—" The eyes lost their focus, the voice wavered.

"Just hang on!" Pryor said quickly. "I'll find the doctor . . ."

Dance managed to shake his head weakly. "No use," he said, and Pryor had to admit that it was probably true. "Not the shape I'm in. They got me good! They . . . shot us all to pieces, Kid."

"I know." Pryor settled back. He knelt there beside his friend, helpless to do anything but watch over him in these remaining moments.

Dance started to cough. A trickle of blood showed at a corner of his mouth. "I couldn't keep up. Couldn't hardly manage that gun-shy, jugheaded bronc—" More coughing, a ragged and painful spasm. "I made it this far," he gasped. "Figured Conchita could help."

"She's not here."

"Just my luck!" Jim Dance grimaced. "Well, luck carried me pretty far. Shouldn't fuss now. We all got to go sometime."

"I'm sorry, Jim!" Pryor told him from the heart. "Except for my interfering, you might . . ."

The fading eyes focused on him again. "Don't blame yourself. It's my fault, Kid. I wouldn't listen to you. I guess—I'm just a poor . . . dumb cowboy who ought . . . to have knowed better—They'll plant me on boot hill. That's all right. Don't make a big thing of it—wouldn't want my friends to say I went out fussing over a bad turn of the cards. Maybe Conchita would bring along her guitar, sing a couple of tunes. She'll know which ones. . . ." The dying man's chest swelled in a last spasm. His features went slack. His eyes closed, the bloody chest stilled. He was gone.

There was the sound of a sob that caused Pryor's head to lift sharply. Conchita stood near them, both hands pressed to her colorless face. Pryor got quickly to his feet.

She crossed herself and fell to her knees. Just at that moment a gust arose to stir the dry weeds and bring them a scorched scent of the far Texas plains, the dark smell of the river, the town odors of dust and horses and of noontime cook fires. And suddenly Pryor had an odd conviction that the old town—this Laredo that had seen so much—had already absorbed the madness of the last week and was starting to settle again into its normal, timeless way of life. Already Jim Dance and Bart

Campion were merging into its past—and, along with them, the ghost of a young fellow who once called himself the Salado Kid.

"It was once in the saddle I used to go dashing,
  Once in the saddle I used to go gay;
First took to drinking and then to card-playing,
  Now I'm shot in the breast and I'm dying today.

"Let six jolly cowboys come carry my coffin,
  Let six pretty maidens come sing a sad song;
Throw bunches of roses all over my coffin,
  And play the dead march as you carry me along."

Oh we beat the drum slowly and we played the fife lowly,
  And bitterly wept as we carried him along,
For we all loved our comrade, so brave, young, and handsome,
  We all loved our comrade although he done wrong.

"The *Stagecoach* series is great frontier entertainment. Hank Mitchum really makes the West come alive in each story."

—Dana Fuller Ross, author of *Wagons West*

STAGECOACH STATION I:

DODGE CITY

HANK MITCHUM

The massive Concord stage thundered across the empty lawless miles of the Great Plains bound for the Wickedest Town in the West—Dodge City. It was a wide-open cattle town always itching for a fight, and a big one was about to start. For Burl Channing was on this stage, a Federal marshall hell-bent on a mission of personal vengeance to bring a vicious murderer to justice. The man he seeks is Frank Killian, a cunning gambler with a killer's finely-honed edge. Frightened of one man and betrayed by the other, Emily Barker, a beautiful young widow, is suddenly caught up in their struggle—a battle that will soon explode in front of the legendary Long Branch Saloon in one of Dodge City's deadliest gunfights.

Buy DODGE CITY at your local bookstore or use this handy coupon for ordering:

★ WAGONS WEST ★

A series of unforgettable books that trace the lives of a dauntless band of pioneering men, women, and children as they brave the hazards of an untamed land in their trek across America. This legendary caravan of people forge a new link in the wilderness. They are Americans from the North and the South, alongside immigrants, Blacks, and Indians, who wage fierce daily battles for survival on this uncompromising journey—each to their private destinies as they fulfill their greatest dreams.

☐	22808	**INDEPENDENCE!**	$3.50
☐	22784	**NEBRASKA!**	$3.50
☐	23177	**WYOMING!**	$3.50
☐	22568	**OREGON!**	$3.50
☐	23168	**TEXAS!**	$3.50
☐	23381	**CALIFORNIA!**	$3.50
☐	23405	**COLORADO!**	$3.50
☐	20174	**NEVADA!**	$3.50
☐	20919	**WASHINGTON!**	$3.50
☐	22952	**MONTANA!**	$3.95

Buy them at your local bookstore or use this handy coupon:

FROM THE PRODUCER OF WAGONS WEST
AND THE KENT FAMILY CHRONICLES—
A SWEEPING SAGA OF WAR AND HEROISM
AT THE BIRTH OF A NATION.

THE WHITE INDIAN SERIES

Filled with the glory and adventure of the coloniza-
tion of America, here is the thrilling saga of one of
the new frontier's boldest heroes. He is Renno, born
to white parents, raised by Seneca Indians, and
destined to be a leader in both worlds. THE WHITE
INDIAN SERIES chronicles Renno's adventures from
the colonies to Canada, from the South to the
turbulent West. Through Renno's struggles to tame a
savage continent and through his encounters with
the powerful men and passionate women on all
sides of the early battles of America, we witness
the events that shaped our future and forged our
great heritage.

☐	22714 White Indian #1	$3.50
☐	22715 The Renegade #2	$3.50
☐	20579 War Chief #3	$3.25
☐	22717 The Sachem #4	$3.50
☐	20028 Renno #5	$3.25
☐	20559 Tomahawk #6	$3.50
☐	23022 War Cry #7	$3.50